Out of
the Blue

OTHER BOOKS BY SARAH ELLIS

A Family Project
Next-Door Neighbors
Pick-Up Sticks

(Margaret K. McElderry Books)

Out of
the Blue

Sarah Ellis

Margaret K. McElderry Books

First United States edition 1995

Margaret K. McElderry Books
An imprint of Simon & Schuster
Children's Publishing Division
1230 Avenue of the Americas
New York, New York 10020

Copyright © 1994 by Sarah Ellis
First published in 1994 by
Groundwood Books/Douglas & McIntyre
Toronto, Canada

The text of this book is set in Sabon.
Design by Michael Solomon

Printed in Canada

10 9 8 7 6 5 4 3 2 1

Library of Congress Catalog Card Number: 94-78090

ISBN 0-689-80025-8

"The Guide Marching Song" by Mary Chater
is reproduced by permission of
The Guide Association (UK).

For Claire Victoria, for later.

CHAPTER ONE

"Then princess mayonnaise pointed her magic wand of power at the bad guys and turned them all into erasers. The end."

Betsy somersaulted out of her beanbag chair and came over to the computer where Megan was typing. "Can you put 'The End' in those fat letters?"

Megan backspaced and pressed the BOLD key. "Okay. Anything else?"

Betsy pointed at the screen. "See where it says 'erasers'?"

"Yup."

"I need some room there so I can draw a picture, in case anyone thinks she changed those guys into shape erasers or neon erasers or sniff erasers. She didn't. She just changed them into dirty old pink erasers. All the same."

"Right," said Megan. "Now we can save." The computer started to zip and bleep.

Betsy hung over the back of Megan's chair. "Did you like that story?"

"Yes, it's good."

"Did you like it better or worse than 'Princess Mayonnaise and the Tooth Fairy'?"

Megan switched on the printer. "Um, I think I like it a bit better."

"Did you like it better or worse than 'Princess Mayonnaise and Her Magic Wings'?"

Megan sighed. Giving a compliment to Betsy was like throwing a stick for Bumper. Once was never enough, and you always got tired of it before they did. "A bit better. Hey, while this is printing, do you want some juice? I'll go get it."

"Sure."

Megan stretched and went upstairs. As she crossed the hall to the kitchen she glanced through the open door into the living room. Mum and Dad were sitting on the couch, their backs to her. Mum's head was bent over a piece of paper.

In the kitchen the dishwasher was draining, doing its swamp monster impersonation, *glug, glug, swish.* Megan opened the refrigerator and took out a box of juice. The dishwasher clunked to a stop and Dad's voice fell into the silence, "Well, if you look at it that way, *everything* is a risk."

Megan closed the refrigerator door quietly and grabbed two glasses from the cupboard. She stood at the living-room door and peeked in at Mum and Dad. Their heads were together now, outlined against the paper.

The printer stopped zipping and Megan went on down to the basement. Betsy was holding a long sheet of computer paper in the air. "Five pages! How many is that all together, Megan?"

"Thirty-eight plus five is forty-three."

"Forty-three! That's way better than Kevin Blandings. He's only got twenty-seven. I've got the longest book in grade two. Is it really good, Megan?"

"It's a great book, Betsy."

"Is it as good as *Mary Poppins*?"

There was only one possible answer. "Yes. Now, you tear off the edges and do the drawing. Don't talk, okay? I've got homework."

Megan turned off the computer and pulled out Betsy's "Mayonnaise" disk. She opened the drawer and filed it away, beside all Dad's stuff, disks marked

"West Coast Foundation Proposal" and "Carswell Mining Annual Report." Dad wrote things for businesses. Some days he put on a suit and went downtown to talk to people in offices. When he came home he usually pretended to hang himself with his tie, and then he would say, "Dynamic and innovative, dynamic and innovative, they all want to sound dynamic and innovative." But most days he stayed home and worked on the computer, writing and making graphs and diagrams.

Megan closed the drawer and picked up her science notebook. Betsy lay on the floor and colored. She held the crayon tight in her fist and scrubbed at the paper. Megan stared at the bright splashes of color. Betsy didn't care about staying inside the lines. Megan pulled her attention back to putting the causes of acid rain into her own words.

Half an hour later Betsy pulled on her sleeve. She made strangling noises through tight-shut lips.

"Okay, okay, you can talk. What is it?"

Betsy pointed to the clock and whispered, "Look! Quarter to nine. They've forgotten to send me to bed."

"You're right. Wonder why." Megan listened carefully and heard the rise and fall of Mum talking upstairs. She realized that Mum and Dad had been talking all evening. It was like becoming aware of a clock ticking. Why wasn't Mum studying? Since she had started college in January she spent most evenings reading and making notes at the kitchen table.

"Let's just keep quiet," said Betsy. "Maybe they won't remember until *midnight*."

The trouble was that after fifteen minutes of keeping quiet, they were both yawning, and midnight seemed a long time away. "Come on," said Megan, pulling Betsy up out of the beanbag chair. "If we're too late, Dad won't read to us."

They made their way upstairs and stood in the doorway of the living room. Mum and Dad were now at opposite ends of the couch, facing each other. Mum's voice had crying in it, "But, Jim, what if it doesn't work out? What if it's a big mis—"

Megan coughed. Mum stopped midword, as though her voice had been snipped with scissors.

"Um, we're going to bed now."

"What?" said Dad. "What time is it? Betsy! You're still up? Come on. We'll have to have a short chapter tonight."

"There aren't any short chapters in Sherlock Holmes," said Betsy with satisfaction, "I looked."

Megan leaned over the back of the couch and kissed Mum. "Good night."

Mum blinked and hugged Megan around the neck too hard.

"Aagh, you're strangling me."

Later, as they were lying in bed listening to Dad read how Sherlock Holmes could tell all kinds of things about a man just by looking at his hat, the front door banged shut.

"What's that?" said Megan.

"Mum must be taking Bumper for a walk," said Dad.

"But she already took him for a walk after dinner."

"Megan!" Betsy bounced up and down on the bed. "Be quiet. It's getting to the part about the diamond."

A few paragraphs later Betsy went from wide-awake to fast asleep, and Dad left Holmes parked in a pub. But Megan coasted along in half sleep for nearly an hour before the front door opened again and Bumper made his way upstairs. Three turns and a snuffle, and he settled down on the rug beside her bed. Everyone home.

The next morning Megan's hair decided to be stupid. By the time she fixed it with mist and the hair dryer she was the last person down to breakfast.

When she walked into the kitchen Betsy was in the middle of a temper tantrum. Mum was standing at the sink washing the porridge pot, ignoring the scene. Dad was being reasonable.

"Betsy, you have to change. You just put your elbow in your porridge bowl. You won't be able to wear your Brownie uniform today."

"But I *want* to wear it." Betsy's face was bright red.

Megan reached into the cupboard for the cereal.

Dad tried adding a suggestion to being reasonable. "Look. We can wash your uniform this evening, and you can wear it tomorrow."

"I want to wear it *today*."

Where was the cereal? Megan tried the pantry cupboard.

Dad tried switching to humor. "Anyway, what would happen if you went to school with porridge on your elbow. People would want to come up and nibble it."

Betsy gave a roar of rage and banged her mug on the table. Humor never worked with Betsy.

"Mum, where's the cereal?"

Mum didn't answer.

"*Mum.*"

Mum turned around and blinked. "What?"

"Where's the cereal?"

"The what?"

What was going on? Did Mum have an exam today or something? Megan spoke slowly and clearly. "The ce-re-al. Cornflakes. In a box."

Betsy was now down on the kitchen floor, sobbing and hiccuping.

"Oh," said Mum, "isn't it in the cupboard?"

"No! I looked there. Never mind. I'll have toast."

Megan put two pieces of toast into the toaster and went to the refrigerator for peanut butter. There was the box of cereal, wedged in between the milk and the juice.

"Hey! Who put the cereal in the refrigerator?"

Betsy jumped up and her tears stopped, like a tap being turned off. "Let's see."

"Oh," said Mum. "I guess I put it there. Sorry. I'm not very with-it this morning."

Dad walked over to the sink and kissed Mum on the neck. They stood there quietly for a few minutes, Dad's blond hair touching Mum's brown, Mum's hands floating quietly in the dishwater. Something was definitely up.

CHAPTER TWO

THE CEREAL DID NOT APPEAR IN THE REFRIGERATOR again, but over the next few weeks Megan noticed a distinct weirdness in the air. And changes. "Minor points in themselves, Watson," said Sherlock Holmes, "but as part of the broader picture I think we can deduce . . ."

Then, one Wednesday morning when Megan came down for breakfast, Mum was still in her housecoat.

"Aren't you going to anthropology?"

Mum's schedule was posted on the refrigerator and they all knew it by heart. And Wednesday was anthropology, first thing.

"No, I'm playing hooky today. Going to lunch with a friend."

But Mum *never* skipped classes, not once in the three months she had been at school. Dad said she must be a professor's dream come true. And "lunch with a friend"? Mum didn't go out for lunch. Between classes she ate the sandwich that Dad packed for her. She didn't go out at all, except for bowling on Friday nights with Aunt Marie.

"I think I'll play hooky too," said Betsy.

"No," said Dad, "only one juvenile delinquent allowed per family."

And then there was the discussion about summer holidays. Betsy arrived home from Brownies crying, holding a notice about summer camp. "It's in July! Finally I'm old enough for sleep-over camp and it's in July."

Megan saw the problem. They always spent the whole month of July at the family cottage on the island. July was their month, and in August the cottage was for Aunt Marie and Uncle Howie and John. How could Betsy even think of missing a week on the island? But Brownie camp—she had been wanting to go ever since she found out that there were special camp badges.

"There's going to be cookouts, and sleeping under the stars one night, and everybody gets to take one stuffed animal. . . ." Betsy's voice was rising and her fists were starting to clench. Bumper began to whimper.

Moments to blast off, thought Megan. She was about to suggest a cookout when they were on the island but Dad interrupted. "No problem. It's going to work out just fine this year. We've decided to switch with Marie and Howie this summer and *we're* going to take August. So Brownie camp will be just fine. That was lucky." He and Mum gave each other gooey smiles.

"Yea! I can go! Sign it, sign it!" Betsy danced around and then plunked the notice on the table.

Megan caught Mum's eye. "Why are we going in August this year?"

"Well, time for a change, we thought. We don't want to get into a rut."

But Mum loved getting into a rut. She liked lists and priorities and things written on the calendar. She said that a solid schedule was the secret of a happy life.

Mum continued, "Besides, we might have something else on in July. We'll talk about it later."

There was a period the size of a basketball at the end of her sentence. The answer that was no answer. What was with all this changing? It was like being

14

on the island ferry when the sea was rough. You weren't sure where the deck was going to be on the next step. This was fun for a little while, but later it made you feel like throwing up. Dad called it "green around the gills."

But the biggest change wasn't a schedule switch or an event. It wasn't a clue from which you could deduce something. It was just Mum. She kept humming all the time, and her eyes would well up with tears for no reason. It was like she had taken off the fast let's-get-things-organized coat that she usually wore, and under it was this soft, slow person. The same person who took care of Bumper when he was a puppy. The same person who would sometimes sing soppy songs like "Whispering while you cuddle near me" with Dad. But now this person was around all the time.

One night, while Dad was reading the last chapter of *The Hound of the Baskervilles*, Mum appeared and said they all had to come to the bathroom to look at the moon. The bathroom was filled with silvery light, and the moon through the window was huge and full.

"Good night for a tramp across the moors," said Dad, who was still in a Sherlock Holmes mood.

"Is it a full moon everywhere at the same time?" asked Betsy. "Like in Africa and Australia. Does everybody get the full moon on the same night?"

"Yes," said Dad. And then he paused. "At least I think so."

"They don't get summer and winter at the same time," said Betsy. "How come they get the full moon at the same time?"

"Hang on," said Dad. He laid out a bar of soap, a rubber dinosaur, and the dental floss on the back of the toilet. "Now, if this is the earth and this is the moon . . ."

But Mum just kept staring up. "Yes, it *is* the same. Anyone looking up in the sky right now sees this full moon. Everyone."

And the tears ran down her face. She hugged Megan around the head. Suddenly the bathroom seemed very small to Megan. There was certainly no space for questions. There was hardly enough space to breathe.

CHAPTER THREE

MEGAN STUCK HER PENCIL INTO THE HOLE IN HER ruler and set the ruler spinning. Today was what Mr. Mostyn called "prewriting." He made them write a story a week, and Monday mornings were prewriting. One month he taught them "webbing," which was putting your ideas in little blobs all over the page and joining them up with lines like a spider web. Another month it was "mapping," which was drawing a road and then arranging your ideas along it. And then there was "brainstorming," which was blurting your ideas out as fast as you could. Megan quite liked prewriting. It was like daydreaming and you didn't have to hand in anything at the end. But this time her mind kept running away from webs and roads, like Bumper avoiding his leash when it was time to go home from the park.

What *was* up with Mum and Dad? It had to be the piece of paper they were looking at, that night on the couch. That was the evening when things had started to go weird. Megan pulled her pencil out of her ruler and wrote "Clues" at the top of her prewriting paper.

1. Mum's remark about things not working out.
2. Dad's remark about everything being a risk.
3. One piece of paper, regular size, white.
4. Change of holiday plans.

She drew a blob around 3. This was the one to pursue. She drew a curving line from the blob to the middle of the page and wrote in capital letters, "FIND IT." She shaded the letters into 3-D while she thought. When? Late at night when everyone was asleep? Too corny. Her stomach rumbled. Of course! Lunch hour. Perfect. She and Betsy always took their lunches to school, but she could make it home and back, and still have time to search if she ran fast. Dad was having a downtown day, so he wouldn't be there. Today was the day.

She scribbled a note.

Dear Erin, Can't have lunch. Going home. Don't mention it if you see Betsy.

She folded the scrap of paper and pushed it across the aisle with her foot. Erin didn't notice. Her head was bent over her paper and she was writing like mad. Megan tried staring at her. *My eyes are boring into your brain.* No response. Erin was really into prewriting. Discreet cough. Erin didn't budge. Megan sliced off a bit of eraser with her fingernail and pinged it at Erin's head with her ruler. Success. Erin looked up indignantly. Megan pointed at the floor. Erin caught on. Message received.

Bumper thought that coming home for lunch was the best idea that Megan had ever had. He woofed and danced around and told Megan, in dog language, that she was the kindest, most brilliant, beautiful and scintillating creature in the known universe, and that he loved her with every fiber of his being. He took some of it back when he realized that he was not going for a walk or getting dinner.

It was funny being in the house alone with just Bumper. Megan felt a bit like a burglar, a nervous burglar. She jumped when the refrigerator turned off with a clunk. Okay. A plan. A piece of paper, with typing or printing on it, folded in three. The coffee table was probably too obvious, but sometimes Holmes had success with the obvious. Not this time. Magazines, flyers, the notice about Brownie camp. Try Mum's desk in the kitchen.

She pulled open the file drawer. Neatly labeled colored files. "Math 115," "Medical," "Megan," "Mortgage." There were far too many. The fattest bunch of papers caught her eye. "To File." She squeezed it out and opened it on the kitchen table. She began to sort through it. Shiny paper, wrong size, colored. She piled up the possibles. Pool schedule, photocopy of a recipe for eggnog cookies, application form for a student loan, a brochure with a picture of a big old-fashioned sailing ship on it — "Tall ships, the experience of a lifetime."

She started to slide it back into the file. Wait a minute. On the back was a photo of a bunch of kids hanging off the rigging of the ship. "For young people aged 12–16. Ply the seas on a replica tall ship, the educational experience of a lifetime. . . . Learn skills of seamanship, self-reliance, and cooperation. . . . July 7–28." Hang on. Who was going to turn twelve in a couple of weeks, on Good Friday? Who couldn't make plans for July?

She scanned the brochure again. "Some sailing experience desirable." Who had taken beginning sailing last summer with her cousin John? Megan felt excitement climbing up her throat. "See enclosed form." She looked carefully through the piles of paper. Gone. They had already mailed it in. They were going to send *her*!

Megan remembered when Emily, her baby-sitter, had gone to England with a choir in grade eleven. Mum said what a great opportunity it was, and how she hoped Megan and Betsy would do a lot of traveling. Three weeks! This very summer! Megan looked more closely at the picture of the kids on the rigging. *Of course* Mum would think it was a risk. But Dad had thought she could handle it. And she could. She pictured herself up in the crow's nest, waving to everyone. Mum and Dad were *the best*.

It must be pretty expensive, though. How could they afford it? Since Mum had quit her job to go to school, she and Dad were always talking about how the mortgage took all their money. Oh, who knows? Megan pirouetted around the kitchen until Bumper barked himself silly and jumped on her. Maybe they had secretly won the lottery. Secret money, secret plans, "the secret of the mysterious summer."

Did you get to sleep in a hammock? She needed to know more about old ships. Was there time to get to the library before one o'clock? She glanced up at the kitchen clock. No way. There was hardly time to get back to school. She gave the brochure one last look, slid the file back into the drawer, grabbed an orange, and gave Bumper two biscuits and a big noisy kiss on the nose. Life was perfect. Life was megaperfect.

Somehow, for the next eleven days, everyone and everything agreed in the megaperfection of life. Dad finished off a big annual report and decided he could take the entire Easter weekend off, four whole days in a row, so they could all go to the island, and Mum promised not to take any homework with her. One day, while fooling around on the mats in gym class, Megan discovered that she could do a perfect front flip. Bumper's flea spray finally kicked in and he stopped scratching. Princess Mayonnaise started a new adventure, with the Easter Bunny, and Betsy named the leader of all the bunnies "Queen Megan." Megan recognized this for the high compliment it was. The weather was warm and soft, and the cherry blossoms drifted into the gutters, like pink snow.

Megan carried the secret of her trip around inside her like a small wrapped present. About a week before her birthday she was surprised to find out that Betsy seemed to know, too. It began with a classic Betsy line while they were getting dressed.

"I know something you don't know."

They had told Betsy. A whole week ahead? That was dangerous. Used to be that Betsy couldn't keep a secret for ten minutes. She stared at Betsy, who was putting on her tights. Maybe Betsy was growing up. Maybe one day she would put her tights on one leg at a time, like a normal person, instead of struggling with both legs at once. The thought of Betsy growing up made Megan feel soft and sad and happy. She smiled.

This made Betsy mad. "Hey! Don't you get it? I know something you don't know."

Megan snapped to attention. She was forgetting her lines. "No way."

"Yes way."

"No way."

"Yes way, yes way, yes way."

Betsy would grow old and grey, she would die of starvation, she would wear out her vocal cords, before she would give up the last word. Megan retreated, "Okay, what is it?"

"Not telling."

Well, obviously. "Is it something to do with my birthday?"

Betsy's face fell. "You guessed."

"It's okay. I didn't guess what. I mean, it's not that hard to guess that it's about a present, but you still know what it is and I don't. Do I get any hints?"

"Maybe, maybe not."

"Is it bigger than a bread box, smaller than a house?"

Betsy smiled a smile of deep satisfaction. "Nope."

"Would somebody please feed that dog. He's scratching the door down." Dad's voice boomed out of the bathroom.

"I'll go," said Betsy.

On her birthday Megan opened her eyes to sunlight shining through the prism in her window. The prism had been a birthday present from Erin, opened one day early. It had rainbows hidden inside it. She stretched her feet down to the end of the bed. Was twelve taller? Would she be the youngest person on the ship? Of course, she wouldn't really have to tell them her age. If they were all strangers, she could be whoever she wanted. She had already pretty well for sure decided that she would say her name was "Meg." "Meg" sounded like a popular person who would never get seasick or homesick. Meg would be good with knots. In fact, Meg sounded a bit like a pirate.

Mr. Mostyn had once read them something about women pirates from long ago. Megan flipped over on her stomach and did a little brainstorming. Meg the pirate was injured in the leg by a cutlass. Cutlass? Was that right? Anyway, she got gangrene in the wound and she had to have the leg amputated, with only a slug of rum for anesthetic. But she was incredibly brave and she got a wooden leg, and from then on she was known as "Peg-Leg Meg."

Waffle-making sounds from downstairs interrupted her brainstorm. She jumped out of bed into her slippers. Forget waiting. Birthday, here I come.

When she came into the kitchen, Megan was surprised to see a pile of presents by her plate and a long skinny wrapped thing leaning against the refrigerator. Presents *and* a trip?

"So," said Mum, kissing her, "how does it feel to be twelve?"

Megan did a fast check of her feelings. "Good," she answered, "really cool." She sat down at her place and rearranged the packages. There it was — the envelope. She would save it for last.

"Waffles first, or presents?" asked Mum.

"Waffles, please," said Megan.

"Oof," Betsy exploded.

"Twelve-year-olds enjoy delayed gratification," said Dad. "I'm sure I read that in a magazine."

Megan had her first waffle with syrup and her second with jam, and couldn't decide which was better. And then it was time.

She reached out for the long thin package. "To Megan, love Daddy."

"Are you going to open your card first?" said Dad.

He was so cute. "No," said Megan, "I don't like that delayed doomathiggy." She ripped open the top of the package and pulled out a canoe paddle. Beautiful shiny blond wood. Carved into the top was a small red flower and her initials.

"My own paddle," she said. "And the flower matches the red canoe." She held it up to her cheek. The wood felt like velvet.

"Dad did the carving himself," said Mum.

Megan leaned across the table and kissed Dad on his sandpapery cheek. She leaned the paddle against the table so she could reach out and touch it.

"Open mine, open mine," said Betsy.

Betsy liked to use lots of tape in wrapping. Megan finally had to cut open the package with scissors. It was a jewelry-making kit, with glass beads and hardware for a necklace, a bracelet, and two pairs of earrings. It was great, except that the earrings were for pierced ears. Probably Betsy hadn't noticed. "Thanks, Bets. That's a great present. I'll take it to the island."

"Did you see what kind of earrings they are?" asked Betsy, looking as though she were going to burst.

"Betsy," said Mum warningly.

What was going on?

"Here," said Mum, pushing a soft package at her. It had a very sweaterlike feel.

It *was* a sweater, dark bluish green and as soft as almost not there. Megan put it on over her pajamas. "I love it."

She took a bite of cold waffle.

"Come *on*," said Betsy, pushing the envelope toward her.

Megan licked the syrup off her knife and used it to slit the envelope. A small plastic bag and a heavy paper certificate fell out. "Redeemable for ear piercing. LaBeaute Nails and Esthetics Salon." Megan emptied the small bag into her hand. A pair of stud earrings, gold with tiny pearls.

"I thought I wasn't allowed to have my ears pierced until I was fourteen."

"The expert persuaded us that we were being hopelessly old-fashioned," said Mum pointing at Betsy.

"That's why the jewelry kit has earrings for pierced ears." Betsy grinned.

"We can make an appointment for you for next week," said Mum, "as soon as we get back from the island. But Dad will have to take you. I can't watch. Too squeamish. Or maybe you would like to go with Erin. . . ."

24   Megan nodded and looked at the table. Where was the other envelope? Then it hit her. There was no

other envelope. These were her presents. These were her great, beautiful presents. There were no tall ships. She had made it up. It was so real and now . . . She tried to keep her face under control, but the tears were welling up.

She pushed back her chair. "Excuse me, bathroom."

She ran upstairs to the bathroom, turned on the tap, hard, and pushed her face into a towel and sobbed. She had been so dumb. How could she have thought . . . They weren't one of those rich families like Emily's. But she couldn't *act* disappointed. She would die if anyone ever found out what she had thought.

She wiped her eyes and looked in the mirror, holding her hair back from her ears, trying to get excited about earrings. It didn't work. It was like somebody had stolen her trip, and that was totally stupid. Disappointment stuck in her throat like a piece of dry waffle. What to do? She splashed cold water on her face. She had to forget it. And until she could forget it, she had to fake it like mad.

CHAPTER FOUR

THEY TOOK THE FERRY TO THE ISLAND THAT EVENING. It was dark by the time they arrived, but a bright full moon had risen. They followed their moon shadows up the road. Betsy got out her flashlight anyway so that she could light her mouth from the inside and make her puffed-out cheeks glow pink. Mum pulled the little wagon they used for carrying stuff from the ferry. Megan balanced her new paddle across her shoulders, making a T shadow on the road. And everyone carefully ignored the fact that Dad was carrying a big white bakery box. A deer leaped out of the ditch and ran across the road ahead of them. Bumper went tearing off after it. A history of total failure in deer chasing did not discourage him. He ambled back a few minutes later. "Deer? I didn't notice any deer."

As soon as they arrived at the cottage Mum lit the kerosene lamp that stood on the big kitchen table. The blue-and-yellow oilcloth glowed. Dad knelt down to the fireplace. "Looks like Howie's been here," he said. "Another architectural masterpiece."

One of the rules of the cottage was that when you left, you made up a fire for the next people. You could always tell when Uncle Howie had been there, because he laid perfect fires, symmetrical kindling like a tepee around a nest of crumpled newspaper and wood shavings, bigger logs ready on the hearth.

"It's almost a shame to burn it up," said Dad, "but I'll force myself." He held a match to a piece of newspaper, and a flame ran along its edge, disappeared for a second, and then sprang up from the kindling. He blew on the flames gently and then hung a kettle of water over the fire.

Mum flipped open the big scrapbook that was sitting on the table. "Yes, Howie was over last weekend. He patched the canoe. He's going to bring some shakes over to fix the roof when they come in July."

Megan pulled her gaze away from the fire. If she wasn't going on the tall ship, what was all that business about changing holidays? "I still don't get it. How come we're not coming in July?"

"Tell you later," said Mum. "Let's get dinner happening."

Megan sat down at the table and looked in the scrapbook to catch up since their last visit. Uncle Josh had been over in February and it had been so cold he'd gone to bed with a plastic bleach bottle full of hot water. There had been a big storm in March. Mr. Thompson, their neighbor on the island, had come over to check things out. Uncle Josh and his friend Mark had visited later that month and they'd gone oystering. They had eaten the oysters raw. Yuck.

Megan pulled a pencil out of her pack and began their entry. "April 10. Hungerfords. Here for the Easter weekend. Deer on Rackham Road. Full moon." Then she slid the scrapbook back into the bookcase, next to all the others, a whole shelf of scrapbooks going right back to when Gram and Pop bought the cabin. On rainy days Megan liked to sit on the saggy couch and read them over. Gram and Pop had died before she was born, but she felt as though she knew them. Pop had stiff, tidy writing, and he liked to record rainfall and wind and the date of the first tomatoes. Gram scrawled, wrote around the edges of the pages, and drew sketches of plants and animals and people. The first entry in the first book, now dog-eared and faded, was signed, "Karl, Trudi, Joshua, Marie, and Snicklefritz." Snicklefritz was Mum before she was born.

So many voices on the pages — kids' names in crayon; poems in the messy writing of some boy-friend of Aunt Marie's before she married Howie; fancy pages for a year or two when Uncle Josh took up calligraphy; thank-you notes from friends who wrote, "This is paradise!"; a months-long discussion of the location for a new outhouse; dates of babies being born and the goldenrod coming into bloom; plans for a monkey puzzle tree at the top of the drive-way; records of the first snowfall of the winter and the last swim of the summer.

Sometimes the older scrapbooks made Megan sad. One of the entries, in Pop's neat black handwriting, said that Gram was "bearing her illness with dignity and grace." It was a good kind of sad.

"Marshmallows!" said Betsy, throwing a bag into the air.

"Yup," said Mum, unwrapping a package of wie-ners. "Fireplace food tonight."

They ate wieners and marshmallows, and then Dad made toast on a stick. It tasted so good with butter and honey that they used up a whole loaf of bread. Mum threw her toasting stick into the fire. "My kind of meal. Burn the dishes."

Betsy and Dad disappeared into the kitchen.

Mum winked at Megan and said in a loud, the-atrical voice. "So—seasonable weather we're having these days, eh?"

Sounds of match lighting and giggling emerged from the kitchen.

28   "Yup," said Megan, "pretty normal, pretty average."

"You can say that again," said Mum, "temperatures just about . . ."

Betsy came around the corner with the cake, singing, "Happy birthday to you. . . ." The light from the candles lit her face from below and she looked like an angel on a Christmas card. They finished singing "Happy Birthday to You," and then Betsy sang the you-belong-in-a-zoo version, and then Dad sang his special birthday song, in his deepest, most tragic voice. He accompanied himself by banging a log of wood on the hearth.

"Hap-py birth-day (thunk),
Hap-py birth-day (thunk),
People are dying everywhere,
Sorrow and sighing fill the air (thunk),
Hap-py birth-day (thunk)."

"You're a bunch of sickoids," said Mum. "Give Megan a chance to wish and blow out the candles before they burn down."

A wish. Megan closed her eyes. She had been thinking about this wish, but now it was hard to put into words. It had to do with things not getting wrecked and used up before she could grow up and see them. Pandas and ozone and . . .

"Hurry *up*," said Betsy.

Megan said it loud and clear in her head. "I wish that things won't be spoiled." She blew out the candles in one swoosh.

"What did you wish?" asked Betsy, ever hopeful that sometime, someone would forget about the secrecy of birthday wishes.

"Not telling."

After cake everyone got the yawns. Megan took the flashlight and stumbled to the outhouse. By the time she got back, Mum had spread out the sleeping bags on the bunk beds. Betsy was already asleep. Megan climbed into her top bunk. She tried to stay afloat, to take out her disappointment and look at it, but she was too heavy with sleep. She sank softly under the surface.

CHAPTER FIVE

"IT'S A JAR. JAM—IS IT JAM OR PEANUT BUTTER?" MUM'S loud voice woke Megan up. She felt her way down the ladder and opened the bedroom door.

Dad was standing next to a big piece of paper pinned to the wall. He was making frantic come-on motions with his hands and pointing with a black crayon to a drawing of a jar and a squidge. Mum and Betsy were yelling.

"What's that blob supposed to be?" said Mum.

Dad added wings to the squidge.

Betsy threw herself back on the couch. "It's a bee —*honey*! Right?"

Dad clapped his hands and pointed a finger at Betsy. He scribbled out the honey pot and started to draw something else.

"Cheese," said Mum. "Honey cheese. What the heck is honey cheese?"

Dad groaned and pointed to the egg timer. There was just a trickle of sand left. He continued decorating the big circle he had drawn on the paper.

"Pizza! Honey pizza. Pizza honey. Don't keep drawing the same thing. Honey pie. Hey! It's honey pie, right?"

Dad shook his head.

"Time!" said Megan.

Dad fell onto the floor and lay with his legs in the air like a dead bug. "Honeymoon. That was the moon. How come everything I draw you guess pizza, Judy?"

"Because everything you draw looks like pizza. Why didn't you draw the moon like a crescent?"

"I was trying to make it look real."

"Weirdo," said Mum.

The whole family was weird as far as Megan was concerned. Pictionary at eight o'clock in the morning? What happened to the concept of sleeping in on weekends?

"My turn," said Betsy. "Going to play, Megan?"

Megan rubbed her eyes and shook her head. She went back into the bedroom and began to pull on her clothes. It felt good to see Mum and Dad being goofy. Since Mum went back to school she was always so busy. Always doing two things at once, like reading while she ironed or making essay notes while waiting in the doctor's reception area. It wasn't all bad. Dad cooked more, which meant pasta instead of all the nourishing food groups. And Mum had less time to notice things like neat rooms. But Megan missed the hanging-out time with Mum, talking to her while she folded laundry, watching bad TV talk shows together. And secretly she liked Mum's taste in books better than the complete Sherlock Holmes.

"Wait till summer," Mum kept saying. "I'll have a nice long holiday and we can get caught up on everything." Megan wasn't sure that everything would keep until the summer.

"It's a boat. No, a shoe. A banana split?" Mum yelled from the living room.

Megan grinned. Whatever the reason, that gooey mood that Mum had been in for the last while seemed to have disappeared. A hopeful sign. She slid her feet into her runners and kicked open the door.

"The agony of defeat," said Dad. "I accept it. I'm going to chop some kindling."

"Good morning, twelve-year-old person," said Mum. "Help yourself to some breakfast."

Megan yawned. Her stomach was still asleep. "Later, okay?" She followed Dad outside and sat on a log. Watery sunshine made its way through thin clouds.

"Now that you're twelve, do you want to learn how to handle an ax?" said Dad.

Megan shook her head. Dad had offered before, but whenever she pictured herself pulling that ax blade down out of the sky, she also pictured it slicing right into her foot. "No thanks, but now that I'm twelve can I canoe in the ocean? I mean, now that I have my own paddle and everything."

Dad parked the ax in the chopping block. "I don't see any reason why not."

Megan woke up. "Really? Now?"

Dad looked out over the water. "Nice calm sea. Sure. Help me take this wood in and we'll get the canoe."

Megan held her arms like a tray and Dad piled wood onto them. Since Dad seemed to be on a yes track she thought she would try something else. "Can I paddle to Pig Island?"

Dad paused for a minute. Megan's arms were starting to break.

"Okay, but you have to stay on this side of the island. It's sometimes choppy on the other side."

"Yea!" Megan tried to dance, but she was too wood laden. So she stagger-danced into the cottage. Pig Island, alone. She had often been there, for picnics, or to go shrimping. But she had always wanted to be there just by herself. Today was the day.

Mum wasn't quite as yesish as Dad. She was full of rules and advice about life jackets, and keeping your weight low and centered in the canoe, and not going beyond the mouth of the bay, all of which Megan already knew. She looked out the front window. The sea was flat as a plate. "I'll be careful."

"Can I come?" asked Betsy.

Megan's heart sank.

"No," said Mum firmly. "Megan will need to concentrate. I'll take you out later if you like."

The whole family came down for the launch. Megan got herself settled. Mum handed her a sandwich. Dad pushed off. A scrape on the sand and then the canoe floated free. Everything that had been heavy and clumsy was suddenly light and graceful. Free, away from the edge of the world. On to China!

It took a few strokes to get the canoe under control. Megan felt bulky in her life jacket, and the canoe kept jiggling. But then her arms remembered what to do and she settled into a rhythm. "Bye!"

"Stay where we can see you," yelled Mum. Bumper ran back and forth along the beach barking his goodbyes.

Megan nodded, dug her paddle in deep, and turned toward Pig Island.

The new paddle was just the right length. Megan's strokes left drippy half-moons on the flat surface of the water. She began to hum quietly, "Dip dip and swing." A sea gull gave a loud "Braaak," and Megan looked up, startled, to see that she was only a few lengths away from the island. It was almost as though she had *thought* herself there.

She pulled the canoe up onto the narrow beach. Oof. She plunked down on the pebbles to catch her breath. What was it about being on a small island? It was like feeling totally safe and private. But more. At home, if you wanted to feel safe and private, you had to go inside walls and locked doors. But on an island you could be safe and free all at once.

Megan jumped up. First thing was to walk right around the island. For today it was hers. She set off clockwise. As soon as the canoe was out of sight Megan began to look for sources of food and shelter. Was twelve too old to play desert island castaway? She picked up a pebble and pitched it as hard as she could into the trees. Oh, who cares? Who would know anyway?

She scrambled along the shore, balancing on rocks and ducking under overhanging bushes. Not too much in the way of berries. It was going to have to be roots and grubs—yuck—until she could plant her own crops.

Hey! This was new. A big overhanging arbutus tree blocked her way. It must have come down last winter. Megan climbed up onto its peeling red trunk and carefully crawled out over the water. Climbing a tree sideways. She gave a tentative bounce and moved forward to where a branch made a secure handhold. She stood up, held on tight, and bounced higher. This was great. She must tell Betsy. Just like a trampoline. She looked down the trunk toward the shore. It would be wimpy to crawl back. She steadied herself on the branch and then ran along the trunk, taking a flying leap across the upturned roots, onto the salal bushes beyond.

As she landed she fell forward and her hand came to rest against something cool and hard. She pulled it out from under the leaves. A Japanese fish float. She stared at the baseball-size glass ball. You *never* found them anymore. It was way above the tide line. Maybe that's why it had been hidden for so long. She held the deep blue glass up to the sun. It would look beautiful beside the shells and driftwood on the windowsill in the cottage. She slipped it into her pocket. It pressed slightly against her hip as she walked. It was like another birthday present, a present from a total stranger.

She came around the final curve of the island and spied the red canoe. She froze with terror. For so many years she had longed for the sight of another human being and now — were they friend or were they foe? And what was that? It looked like a paper bag that probably contained a sandwich. So welcome after years of grubs.

Megan carried her lunch and her life jacket along the beach to a chairlike rock at the water's edge. She took off her shoes and put her feet in the water. A pale line moved up and down her ankles with the rise and fall of the gentle waves. She wiggled her toes in the cold, leaned back against her life jacket, and unwrapped her sandwich.

She stared at the canoe. A short ship if there ever was one. But there was something good about being totally in control. Probably on that tall ship thing you had to just do what you were told. Was there one part of her that was a bit relieved not to have to face all those older kids she didn't know? Maybe. Anyway, the important thing was that nobody had guessed what she had been thinking. What if she had told Erin or John? She felt hot just imagining it. She adjusted her life-jacket pillow. Keeping quiet — that had been her life jacket. Maybe she had sort of capsized, but she hadn't drowned.

CHAPTER SIX

"Lupper!" Mum was standing by the stove.

"Lupper?" said Betsy.

"Well, if you can have brunch, I don't see why you can't have a late afternoon meal called lupper," said Mum. "I don't know about everyone else, but I'm starving. This island air."

After a lupper of chili and more birthday cake Betsy wanted to play another round of Pictionary, but Dad said no. "Not now, Bets," he said. "Mum has something she wants to talk about. Come sit by the fire. I'll get the tea, Judy."

Betsy snuggled in between Mum and Dad on the lumpy couch, and Megan sat on the floor and poked a stick into the fire. Maybe she could take the canoe out again tomorrow.

Mum cleared her throat. "I have something to tell you girls, and it's a little hard to talk about." Her voice squeezed shut.

Megan turned around from the fire. Since they had come to the island, Mum had been normal again. What was up now?

"Good or bad?" said Betsy, sitting up straight.

Mum laughed a little. "Good, yes, most definitely good."

Hope bubbled up in Megan. Had they saved her final birthday present until now? Was the trip really going to happen after all?

Mum blew her nose. "A long time ago, when I was just a teenager — seventeen — I had a baby, a girl. I was too young to care for her, so I gave her up for adoption. I've never told you about this because . . . well, it was very private, and sad for me. And I wasn't sure you would understand until you were older."

Mum took a deep drink of tea, like someone gulping air. It was so quiet they could hear her swallowing.

"It was a very hard thing to decide when I was that age. And I have always wondered about her. How did she grow up? Was she happy? And so, a couple of years ago, I put my name down at a registry where adopted children can find their birth parents if they want to. And about a month ago I received a letter from her. And we met. . . ." Mum's voice was getting thinner and thinner. She drank more tea. "And we met, and now she would like to get to know the rest of the family. And I would like that, too."

There was a long pause. "Her name is Natalie." Dad reached across Betsy and took Mum's hand.

"Is she my age?" said Betsy. "Would she play with me?"

Mum smiled. "No, she was born long before you, Betsy, long before Megan. She's twenty-four years old and she's going to be married this summer, in early July. She wants us to come to the wedding. I think that's why she decided to try and find me. Getting married makes you think about. . ."

"Your ancestors," said Dad.

Megan was so full of confusion that she felt her edges disappearing, like a cloud. Then a twig snapped in the fire and she jumped back into herself. She picked a question out of the messy pile in her mind. "How come you got pregnant when you didn't want a baby?"

38 Mum swallowed and sat up straighter. "I didn't use birth control."

"But *why* didn't you?"

"Oh, Megan, it's complicated. Rob came along and he played the guitar and he was older and. . . . Somehow I thought it would never happen to me."

What did guitar playing have to do with it? And "complicated." That's not how Mum had described sex and all that before. Had she been lying?

"Has she been to our house?" said Betsy. "Has she seen our room?"

"No, we decided to meet for the first time in a restaurant. That turned out to be not such a hot idea because we both kept crying."

Right, Megan thought, lunch with a friend.

"Yes," said Dad, "from what I've gathered they cried into their soup, and then they cried into their cheesecake, and then they cried into their coffee, and didn't eat anything."

"Why were you sad?" said Betsy.

"Not sad," said Mum, "happy."

"I don't cry when I'm happy," said Betsy.

"No," said Mum with a smile, "it's one of the weird things grown-ups do."

This was all becoming too unreal. Megan needed to know. "Didn't you *want* to keep the baby? Lots of kids have only one parent."

"Yes, part of me did want to keep her. I even bought little things, socks, and put them away. But at the same time, I knew I couldn't really be a mother, not the right kind. There was a sad, regretful place in me for years. It didn't go away until I had you."

"Me?"

"Yes, as soon as I held you, right after you were born, that little sad knot just melted away. Because then I knew I could be a real mother."

"Is she my sister or my cousin?" said Betsy.

"Sister — well, half sister."

"When's her birthday? Did you ask her?"

"September 28." Mum's voice got thin again. "I didn't have to ask."

Betsy nodded. "Now can we play Pictionary?"

"Let's save it till tomorrow," said Dad. "But we could use a little wood. Want to come down to the beach with me and help collect it?"

"Sure," said Betsy.

Megan and Mum sat quietly as Dad and Betsy left. Megan stared into the fire. Mum's hand came down on her shoulder. "Are you all right?"

"I don't know."

"It's a shock, I realize. I tried to think of how to tell you so it wouldn't be out of the blue. But it *is* just out of the blue."

Mum's hand was heavy on Megan's shoulder, and annoying. "I just want you to know—I like Natalie a lot and I hope you will, too, but she isn't my daughter the way you and Betsy are."

Well, obviously.

"I've been thinking about this a lot, since I met Natalie. It's like with her I had the first couple of pages and now I'm jumping into the middle of chapter eleven or something. But with you and Betsy we're in the whole story together. I mean, you and I have twelve whole chapters called "Christmas Morning." And then there's "Chicken Pox" and "Soccer Triumph: Megan's Winning Goal." Not to mention "What Really Happened to Gerald the Gerbil and Why We Can't Tell Betsy."

How obvious could you get? Mum was trying to get her to laugh. Well, forget that.

"If you want to ask me anything . . ."

Megan sat still as a stone, and Mum squeezed her shoulder and then removed her hand. "Do you want to go help Dad?"

A fog of tiredness settled on Megan. "No, I think I'll go read."

Mum kissed her on the top of her head. "Okay."

Megan took *The Secret Garden* into the upper bunk and read until the light grew dim. She could hear Betsy talking nonstop in the next room. Surely it was time for bed. She made the trek to the outhouse and then got a mug of water from the bottle next to the sink. She took her toothbrush to the open window near the stove. Spitting out the window was one of the best of the island traditions. She glanced over to the fire where Betsy was sitting, poking the coals with a stick. Mum and Dad were sitting at opposite ends of the couch.

About a month ago I received a letter. Mum and Dad on the other couch, Mum holding that piece of paper. And what had Dad said? "Anything is a risk." A risk. The risk of high seas and the mainmast snapping in a storm. Megan spit toothpaste water out the window. Her disappointment came flooding back. How could she have been so *wrong*? Megan Hungerford—girl detective. More like girl stupido-head. Tall ships. Move that idea right into the little garbage can. Instead pick option B—a total stranger moving into your life. She flung the rest of the water out into the trees. "We're in the whole story together." Well, not quite. What about the chapter called "Birthday Wrecked, Trip Stolen"? All by this Natalie person.

"When is Natalie coming to our house?" said Betsy.

"I've invited her for dinner a week from Sunday," said Mum.

"Can Auntie Marie and Uncle Howie and John come, too?"

"I think we'll be enough to cope with the first time," said Mum with a grin. "Although Marie is so curious that I wouldn't be surprised to see her hidden in the hedge with a periscope."

Megan turned around from the window. "You told *Marie* before you told us?"

"Yes, when I was trying to decide what to do I needed to talk to someone who knew me when I was seventeen and knew the background to the story. There isn't really anyone except Marie and Josh. And Josh . . . well, it isn't something to talk about long distance."

"Who else knows?"

"Just Marie and Howie. I asked them not to tell John until I had talked to you."

"So now are you going to tell *everyone*?"

"Well, I'm not going to hire a skywriter," said Mum, "but I don't see any reason to keep it a secret. I'm sick of secrets."

Yeah, right. Sick of secrets now. Keeps something a secret from her own children and then decides to broadcast it. Betsy would probably announce it in school. It was all going to be totally embarrassing. Well, one thing was for sure. Nobody was going to hear it from her.

Later, in bed, Betsy just wouldn't shut up. Her voice from the bottom bunk was as insistent as a mosquito's whine.

"She probably wears makeup. I mean she's a grown-up. Mum doesn't wear makeup, but I think our sister will. Maybe she'll let us try it on. Do you think so? Hey! Hey, Megan, do you think so? Are you asleep?"

Megan's top-bunk mattress began to bounce up and down. "Betsy, get your feet off the bottom of my bunk."

"Okay. What do you think? Long hair or short hair? I hope it's long. I hope she's pretty."

"Oh, good grief. She's not a Barbie doll, you know."

Betsy giggled. "You're funny. A Barbie doll! I know that. I know she's a human being. Maybe she'll come and live with us. Oh no, I forgot, she's going to get married. So she'll go and live in her own house. But I'll bet she has us for overnights sometimes. . . ."

Megan lay curled up and quiet and, at long last, Betsy dropped off to sleep in the middle of a word.

Finally, space to think. Some room to take out her tangled thoughts and have a look at them. Megan stretched out long and stiff in the bed and reached her arms up to press against the roof. A lie. Mum and Dad had been lying to her for years. Maybe not in words but in silence. "Just tell the truth," they always said, "even if you've done something wrong. In the long run it gets you into less trouble than lying, and you don't have to carry the lie around." Yeah, right. Good advice from liars. What else had they lied about? Why should she believe them about anything?

Megan's arms and legs felt as though they would explode if she had to lie in bed one more minute. She stuck her head over the side of the bunk and listened to Betsy. Deep, regular breathing. She was gone. Carefully Megan stuck her feet out and found the rungs of the ladder. She climbed down, front side forward. Her toes curled on the cold linoleum. She touched the back of the door and felt something soft, somebody's jacket or robe. She pulled it off the hook, opened the door, and stepped out into the living room.

The dying fire lit the room softly. The door to the big bedroom was closed. Good. She looked at what she had grabbed. Uncle Howie's kangaroo jacket. She pulled it over her head. It was as long as a dress. The sleeves hung down like flippers. She crawled into a corner of the couch, stretched the soft fabric over her knees, and pulled up the hood. It smelled like seaweed and smoke.

She stared through the screen into the fire. The worst thing was the way Mum seemed to expect her to be, like, thrilled. And they were so happy with the way Betsy was acting. When it was only that Betsy was too dumb to get it. Well, forget thrilled. She wasn't thrilled. She wasn't thrilled and she wasn't going to lie about it. She would be polite. She wasn't about to sulk or have a Betsy-style tantrum. It wasn't worth the effort. But this Natalie person was not her sister. She was just an accident. Why did you have to include an accident in your family?

The firelight played over the scrapbooks in the bookcase. Would Natalie want to come here? Would she be writing in the book? Maybe she would want to bring her husband when they were married. Maybe they would have a baby, and it would be one of the births recorded. Hey, hold it, was there anything . . . ?

Megan did some arithmetic. If Natalie was twenty-four years old, then she was born in September of . . . Megan pulled her arms out of the flipper sleeves and reached over to the bookcase. That was too early. Here it was. Surely there would be some hint. She turned the pages. Records of storms and seal sightings, recipes, some driftwood sketches that Gram had made. On the day Natalie was born, some family called the Gills had been for the weekend and had fed lettuce to the rabbits. Nothing. So these books were a lie, too. All that stuff just closed over the top of what had really happened and hid it.

Megan let the book fall to the floor. *Fwap*. She hunched down in her jacket and listened. But there was no noise from the big bedroom. There was no noise at all. Just the sound of ash falling in the fire, a whispering sound, a sound like a secret.

CHAPTER SEVEN

Tuesday morning before school Megan phoned Erin to book her for recess. Erin wasn't sure. "I wanted to play volleyball."

"Forget volleyball. I need to talk to you."

"What's happening?"

"Tutankhamen's tomb." Tutankhamen's tomb was a code reserved for serious occasions. It meant, "Can't talk now. Parents might be listening."

"Okay, see you later."

Erin was so amazed by Megan's news that she stopped eating her cookie in midchew. Erin never forgot about food. "Wow. You're so lucky."

Lucky? "I don't see what's lucky about it."

"Getting to have an older sister. You know Tyler in Mrs. Frame's class? He has this older sister, from when his dad was married once before, and she lives in California and he got to go there for the whole of spring break."

"That's completely different. He's known about her for his whole life, right? Not like some surprise. This Natalie could be a space alien, for all I know."

"So when do you get to meet her?"

"She's coming for dinner a week from Sunday, and Mum spent the whole weekend talking about it. Like the queen is coming or something."

"Aren't you just dying to see what she looks like?"

"No, not really. Why would I be?"

"To see if she looks like *you*, space case."

"I hadn't thought of it. She's not going to look like me. She's old. After all, she's about to get married."

"Will you get to go to the wedding?"

"Mum said we were invited."

"Oh! Weddings are so great."

"Have you been to one?"

"Yeah, my uncle Dave's. The summer after fourth grade. We drove to Saskatchewan. It was the best time. We stayed in this big motel and all the adults got really silly. On the day of the wedding we were walking up the street toward the church, and Mum was walking with Uncle Barry, and we passed this lawn sprinkler. And Uncle Barry said, 'I dare you to run through the sprinkler,' and Mum just gave him this look and put her purse down on the sidewalk and ran right through it. I couldn't believe it. She sat all through the wedding with water polka dots all over her. Uncle Barry told me that when they were kids they had to be careful what they dared Mum to do because she would *always* do it.

"And after the wedding in the church there was this big party and Uncle Dave polkaed me so fast he lifted me right off the floor. Even after Uncle Dave and Monique left, in their honeymoon clothes, people kept eating and drinking and dancing. Everyone forgot about us. Nobody made us go to bed. Some little kids just fell asleep under the tables. I'd love to go to another wedding."

"You can go to this wedding disguised as me. I don't want to go."

"You're crazy. Weddings have great food."

"Can we talk about something else?"

"Okay. What's Natalie going to call your mum — 'Mum'?"

"No way! She already has a mother. You can't just go calling somebody 'Mum.' Besides, didn't I just say could we talk about something else?"

"I thought you meant something else other than weddings. I didn't know you meant something else other than the whole subject. Anyway, don't get mad. *You're* the one who Tutankhamened *me*, remember?"

Erin was right. Why get mad? It was just that . . . All she knew was that she didn't want congratulations. "You're right. I'm sorry. Hey, I almost forgot to tell you. I get to have my ears pierced. Want to come?"

"Sure."

Megan pulled out her apple. "Are you mad?"

"No. I just don't get it." Erin noticed the forgotten cookie in her hand and took a big bite.

That was it. That was the problem. Erin didn't get it. Betsy didn't get it. Mum didn't get it. Nobody got it. She hardly got it herself.

After Erin's reaction Megan didn't feel like telling anyone else the news. Not that she needed to. Mum was doing a good job spreading the word. She was always on the phone, talking about Natalie. She said the same things over and over. She might as well have put it on the answering machine.

"Yes, a great surprise but such a happy one."

"Studying for a PhD in astronomy at the university —sure didn't get those brains from me."

"No, it is like we've known each other for years, right from the first moment."

It was better to be out of the house. Saturday morning Megan woke up to the sound of Mum already on the phone. She could tell by Mum's voice that this time it was *to* Natalie, not *about* her. That was the worst. During these conversations Mum's face sort of melted and her voice went all soft and mushy. She laughed a lot, as though Natalie was some sort of comedy star. But when she repeated her remarks later, and she always did repeat them later, it was just ordinary boring stuff. When she hung up she would sit and sigh. It was revolting.

Megan nearly turned over and went back to sleep when she remembered Art Experience. Today was the first day of the latest class that Mum and Aunt Marie had cooked up for her and John. Well, mostly Aunt Marie. Mum and Dad weren't that big on classes and lessons. But Aunt Marie wanted John to widen his horizons, explore new areas and be well-rounded. Aunt Marie wanted John to be exposed to the many facets of our rich world. That's the way Aunt Marie talked. Trouble was, John refused to go to anything by himself. So Megan usually got roped in.

She didn't really mind expanding her horizons. Some of the classes had been good, like group guitar and Slugs and Bugs. And if Art Experience would get her out of the house for the morning, she was grateful.

She met John in the lobby of the art school. They were early. There was a whiteboard sign with all the classes listed. John found their listing: "Art Experience, Rm. 210, J. Evans."

"I wonder what J. Evans is like?"

"Probably wears a beret," said Megan, "and a big beard."

"And a long shirt not tucked in," said John.

"As long as he's not like Mr. Daynard."

"Aagh," said John strangling. "Remember 'Deeper! Richer! Wider'!"

"He was a nut," said Megan. Mr. Daynard had taught Creative Drama, and he always wanted them to be deeper, richer, and wider when they were just trying to remember their lines.

John looked at his watch. "I think we can go now."

J. Evans turned out to be a she, with plain brown hair and a regular dress. She looked like somebody's mother. She told them they should just wander around and look at things for a few minutes. The room was like a treasure house. There was so much of everything — rolls of paper and big tins of paint, jars of colored pencils, blocks of clay, rolls of wire, big brushes. Megan took a deep whiff of the dusty smell of paper and the sharp smell of paint.

The project for the day was to create an imaginary garden, with flowers and animals and insects that you just made up. Megan started with a pencil and drew a huge flower with every petal different. Then she switched to pencil crayons. They were the good kind that spread their colors like butter. As she concentrated on filling the shapes with scarlet lake and burnt umber, her fingers remembered the pleasure of coloring in the pictures of her second grade workbook. She wasn't like Betsy. She liked staying inside the lines.

The rhythm and concentration of coloring made Megan feel as though she were living inside her space-alien flower and as though everything else had disappeared. She was startled when J. Evans came around to collect the pictures.

"Look at this wonderful variety of styles." J. Evans tacked the pictures to the corkboard. Two girls called Anna and Su-Lin had worked in pastels and their gardens were beautiful. They were obviously going to be the stars of Art Experience.

John had concentrated on a pencil drawing of one insect. He had erased so many times that his paper had holes in it.

"Tell us about this," said J. Evans.

"It's a Venus peopletrap," said John. "It traps people and then digests them with its special human-dissolving saliva."

Anna and Su-Lin broke into "eeeeoooo" noises and "Oh, gross." But J. Evans just smiled. "I like the way you've made the mechanics very clear."

Then, oddly enough, it was Megan's picture that J. Evans decided to concentrate on. "See how Megan has outlined all her shapes, like a coloring book?"

Megan started to get nervous. She knew you weren't supposed to like coloring books, in case they stifled your creativity. But J. Evans didn't seem to care about that. "Many artists have been fascinated with the idea of blocks of contained color." She pulled out some art books and showed them pictures of paintings like quilts and checkerboards. Megan liked them. They were very tidy.

"Try to imagine this one huge," said J. Evans, pointing to a picture of a single red square, "as big as that wall." She turned to the front. "Oh, no, is it noon already? Time is a tyrant. Okay, here's your thought for the week. Lines are just pretend. There aren't any lines in nature, just edges, the edge of one color and the beginning of another. So next week we're going to forget all about line and color and get out the clay. See you then. Remember to look around you."

It had begun to pour while they were in their class, and John phoned his dad to see if he could come and get them. They waited in the lobby and looked out the window. The blossoms lay soggy in the gutter.

"Okay," said John, "what's this about a sister?"

Megan's stomach tensed up. For a whole morning she had forgotten about Natalie. "Half sister."

"Whatever. Mum told me a little bit. When do you get to see her? Is she really an astronomer?"

"She's an astronomer student. And she's coming for dinner a week from tomorrow."

"Do you think you're going to like her?"

"What's to like? She's a perfect stranger."

"But she's your sister. Okay, half sister. I mean, aren't you curious? Like, *bam!* all of a sudden there are three kids in your family."

"She's not a kid. She's twenty-four."

"You know what I mean. Are you excited?"

"I don't need to be. Mum and Betsy are excited enough for our house."

John stood in the doorway and tried to push the frame apart. "This means I have another cousin. She won't be my oldest cousin, though. That's Murray the Mountie from Manitoba."

"She's only your half cousin."

"Whatever. Do you know what she drives?"

"I don't even know if she has a car. I don't really care."

John got a thoughtful look on his face. "You know, she's not my half cousin. She's my whole cousin."

"She is not. She's my half sister, so she's your half cousin."

"No, look." John started to draw a diagram on the misty window. Across the top were Marie and Judy and Josh. Three little lines came down from Judy, one from Marie, and none from Josh. "Okay. Now, the reason we're cousins is because your mum and my mum are sisters. It doesn't matter who your dad is, or mine. Therefore, Natalie is just as much a cousin to me as you are."

Megan reached up with her jacket sleeve and wiped out her family. John was right. Right and totally wrong. Add him to the list of those who didn't get it. Oh good, there was Uncle Howie. "Look, there's your dad. He's stopped in the bus zone. Hurry!" They pulled their jackets up over their heads and ran out into the teeming rain.

CHAPTER EIGHT

Mᴜᴍ ᴇᴍᴇʀɢᴇᴅ ꜰʀᴏᴍ ʜᴇʀ ɴᴀᴛᴀʟɪᴇ ᴅᴀᴢᴇ ʟᴏɴɢ enough to remember about Megan's ear piercing. She made an appointment for Thursday after school. All week long Megan obeyed J. Evans's instructions and looked around her, at ears. At first she just surveyed pierced and nonpierced. But then she started noticing the variety of ears. By Wednesday everyone's ears were starting to look extremely strange. It was like saying a word over and over again until it sounds like nonsense. After five days of observation all ears looked like tide pool creatures glued to the sides of people's heads.

Erin was very happy to go with Megan. "Any chance they'll give you a general anesthetic?" she asked hopefully.

"Erin! This is ear piercing, not surgery."

"I know," said Erin sadly. "I'll never get to see surgery. It's not fair. If you want to be a librarian, you can join the Future Librarians Club and you get to go downtown and visit behind the scenes at the central library. But if you want to be a doctor, there's no Future Doctors Club and no way to get into an operating room."

Mum picked Megan and Erin up at school the following Thursday and drove them to the mall. "I really can't come into the beauty shop with you," she said. "You know me. Will you be okay with Erin?"

"Sure," said Megan.

"It's good premedical experience," said Erin.

"Yes," said Mum. "I remember when you wanted that plastic woman model for your birthday when you were, what was it, six? Have you still got it?"

"The amazing transparent woman? No," said Erin, "she broke after I operated on her to remove her appendix. I wish you could buy one made with some kind of soft plastic that you could cut into. . . ."

"Enough!" said Mum with a shudder. "We're a bit early. Do you want to have a snack before the deed is done?"

"Yes, please," said Erin. "They have a great cinnamon bun place in this mall."

They were licking their buttery, cinnamon-syrupy fingers when a man came up to Mum and said shyly, "Judy Schlegel?"

Mum turned her head to the side. "Ye-es." Then she grinned. "It can't be. Randy Fuller? Mrs. Ironsides's fifth grade, right?"

Megan rolled her eyes at Erin. Mum had lived in the same neighborhood her whole life and was always meeting people from the olden days. It was boring. Any minute now Mr. Fuller would say, "You haven't changed a bit." She concentrated on unrolling her last spiral of bun.

". . . so I just have the one boy and he lives with his mother. Do you have any other children besides Megan?"

"Yes, I have . . ." There was a pause. Then Mum continued, "two other girls. Three wonderful daughters."

Megan put down her remnant of bun. It was too sweet. The cinnamon smell was thick around her. What did they do, pump cinnamon perfume into the air?

"Here's my card," said Mr. Fuller. "We should get together sometime. Bring the family over for a barbecue or something."

"Yes, let's do that. Nice to see you, Randy. You look just the same as in fifth grade." Mum stood up. "Okay, girls, we'd better go."

They set off toward the ear-piercing store.

"Are you going to get together with that man again?" asked Megan.

"Probably not," said Mum, "given how busy everyone is."

"But you said you would."

"I know, but that's just a way of ending the conversation."

"So you were lying."

"It's not lying, it's . . . well, it's a convention."

Megan pressed her mouth shut. It was lying. Funny how she had just started to notice how grownups lie all the time. Like, if Mr. Fuller looked like that in Mrs. Ironsides's class, he must have been a pretty strange fifth-grade kid.

Mum left them at the receptionist's desk at La-Beaute Nails and Esthetics, and a young woman in a blue smock took them into the back room. There was a row of chairs and two other customers. One was a woman with a towel turban and a green face. Bright green, all over, except for an oval around her mouth and two eyeholes. She was leaning back and she looked asleep.

The other customer was a woman sitting on a couch with her bare feet propped on cushions. Her toenails were painted bright pink and the toes were spread apart with cotton balls. She was reading a book.

"Loretta will be with you in a minute," the smock lady said. "You can sit right here."

Megan looked at Erin, who looked back with a "yikes" look and then leaned over and whispered, "Those feet look like hands."

Megan glanced over to the couch and saw it immediately. Two long skinny hands with little stubby fingers all spread out like someone saying "Stop!" Giggles bubbled up from the bottom of her stomach. She tried to turn them into coughing. The woman with the toes glared at them over her book. Erin, the brat face, just sat calmly looking into space.

Loretta appeared with a little wheeled table. "Hi, girls. Who's the one for ear piercing?"

Megan pushed the giggles back into her throat. "Me."

"Great. Do you have your studs? Perfect. Oh, aren't they pretty? Big day, eh? I remember when I first had my ears done."

Loretta talked on as she dabbed something cold onto Megan's earlobes, and then she took a towel off the table and under it was a gun. ". . . so we just fit these studs right in here. . . ."

Megan's giggles evaporated. The gun looked so serious and it felt heavy as Loretta fitted it around Megan's ear. "Ready to go?"

Megan glanced at Erin, who was staring hard. "Okay."

There was a loud crack and a red-hot arrow shot through Megan's ear. It seemed to carry on right into the back of her throat. She grabbed the sides of her chair and screwed her eyes shut against the tears. Why had nobody told her how much this hurt?

"Oh, dear," said Loretta, "you're as white as a sheet. Was it bad?"

Megan nodded her head, once.

Loretta dabbed Megan's ear with something that stung. "For most people it's just not that painful, but for some it is. Sorry, sweetie. Do you want to go ahead with the second ear or not? You don't have to."

Megan knew that if she thought about it she would say no, so she quickly nodded. "Yes."

"Just remember to keep breathing."

The cold liquid on her second ear gave Megan goose bumps, like the gentle brush of a wasp's wings before it stings. And then another crack. She didn't remember to keep breathing.

"There we go," said Loretta. "Now you've got holes in your head. Ha-ha, just a little ear-piercing joke."

Megan glanced at the used cotton balls sitting on the table, each with its little smear of blood. Her fingers felt hollow. What was inside there, inside her earlobe? Little baggies of blood? Erin would know. Megan didn't think she would ask. It was better for the inside stuff to just stay inside, and for her not to think about it. She stared at the line of her arm against the chair and tried not to cry. Of course, it wasn't a line at all. Just an edge, the edge between Megan and not-Megan. Inside, outside, and edge. And unless you were the amazing transparent woman, all people saw of you was the edge.

". . . turn them three times twice a day, and if you're careful, you shouldn't have any problems." Loretta reached over and patted Megan's arm. "Feeling better now?"

Megan nodded. She hadn't heard one word of Loretta's instructions. What if she did something wrong and her ears got infected and fell off? She reached up to touch them, earlobes and earrings, hot and cold, Megan and not-Megan. It was okay. No doubt Erin had listened to the whole thing and would be able to offer paramedical advice. Megan stood up and thanked the outside edge of Loretta. The pain had dulled to a throb. Green Face and Glamour Feet sat unmoving. Time to go and exhibit her ears to the outside edge of Mum.

CHAPTER NINE

THE DAY BEFORE NATALIE'S VISIT MUM WAS CLEANING the bathroom window frame with a Q-Tip when Megan left for Art Experience. When she got home from Art Experience, Mum was vacuuming the kitchen drawers. Megan went upstairs to escape, only to discover that Mum had rearranged the stuff in her room. She arranged everything right back to where it had been.

That evening Mum washed the light fixtures. She was standing at a sink full of suds when Megan walked by.

"What are you doing, Mum?"

"I'm just washing the glass shades. They get all this greasy dust on them up there on the ceiling."

Megan pulled herself up onto the counter. "Mum, how tall is Natalie?"

Mum turned around smiling. "Oh, she's just exactly the same height I am. We stood back to back and there was not a smidge of difference. She's slimmer, though."

Megan slid off the counter. This was hopeless. What had gotten into Mum? The question about Natalie's height had been sarcastic. How tall is Natalie, like, is she going to walk into the house and see the tops of the light fixtures? Get it? Not only did Mum not get it, but she gave that sick oh,-good,-Megan-is-taking-an-interest-in-Natalie smile. The voice in Megan's head took off. Who cares how slim

Natalie is? Tell me about something interesting, like the life cycle of a newt.

She noticed Mum's "To File" folder on the kitchen counter. Oh yes, important to get all the filing done before Natalie arrived. She suddenly remembered the tall-ships brochure and flipped through the file. It was still there. She pulled it out.

"Hey, Mum, what's this?"

"What?" Mum turned from the sink and glanced at the brochure. "Oh, some program to send inner-city kids on a sailing expedition. I think I sent them a donation. Why?"

"Nothing." Megan tossed the paper back into the file. That was the end of that story.

Megan wandered back to her room. This whole thing was turning Mum strange. All week she had been either polishing doorknobs or discussing the menu for dinner. In the middle of a normal conversation she would suddenly say, "Which do you think is better with chicken — rice or mashed potatoes?" Not a word about her religious studies term paper or her psychology midterm. Megan thought about what would happen if *she* started to ignore her homework.

It would be good to get this dinner over with. Surely they wouldn't have to keep seeing this Natalie over and over again. She would, Megan hoped, come and enjoy the rice (or mashed potatoes), be impressed by how clean the cutlery drawer was, tour the house with Betsy (big thrill), and then leave. And then they could get back to normal.

On Sunday, dinner preparations were complete by one o'clock in the afternoon. Natalie was due to arrive at six. Open-heart surgery could have been performed in any room of the house, they were so clean. The table was set. There was a bowl of deluxe mixed nuts on the coffee table, with the phone book balanced on top to keep Bumper from discovering them. The parts of the salad were in plastic bags in the refrigerator. There was a tape in the tape deck. Mum was wearing a dress. Betsy was wearing her Brownie uniform. The only thing left for Mum to do was change her mind.

"Do you think this necklace is too dressy?"

"I wonder if we need another cooked vegetable?"

"I sure hope Jim remembers to bring home club soda. Maybe I should go down to the corner and get some, just in case."

Megan had to escape. She took her bike down to the library to check out the videos. On a wet Sunday afternoon the only videos left were ones that are good for you. But even *Safety in the Home* looked interesting when the alternative was Mum. She was in the basement learning about smoke alarms when the doorbell rang. Six on the dot. Suddenly her heart began to pound. What was going on? Dinner with a stranger, that's all it was. She gave Bumper a vigorous scratch around the ears and then headed firmly upstairs.

By the time she got to the front hall, it was already packed: Mum, Dad, and Betsy all crowded around. There was hugging, more crying on Mum's part, Natalie's dripping umbrella to be taken care of, her coat to be hung up. After being introduced Megan climbed halfway up the stairs to be out of the way. She stared. Natalie was wearing a short skirt and one of those square jackets with big shoulders. Her legs were skinny all the way up. She had short, smooth, dark brown hair and a wide mouth. She didn't look like Mum. Maybe it was a mistake.

Natalie was just leaning over to take off her boots when Bumper came bouncing up from downstairs. He had been in all day because of the rain and he was even more excited than usual to have a visitor. He joined the mob in the hall, and before anyone could grab him he jumped up on Natalie. She turned white and made a little strangled noise in her throat. And then she kicked Bumper. Megan froze on the stairs. Nobody else had seen the kick. They had been too close.

"Off, Bumper," said Dad in his dog-training voice that never worked. "Come on, boy." He grabbed Bumper by the collar. "Sorry about that," he said to Natalie.

"It's okay," said Natalie in a tight voice. "I should have mentioned it. I'm just . . . Well, I don't take to dogs."

"No, no," said Mum, "I should have mentioned that we have one. Megan, would you take Bumper to the basement?"

Megan dragged Bumper off, through the kitchen and toward the basement door. She held him tight at the top of the stairs. "She kicked you. I hate her."

She went down to the basement and threw Bumper his slimy tennis ball a couple of times.

"Megan!" Mum called her from upstairs.

Megan trudged back up. In the living room Betsy was sitting close to Natalie on the couch. "Did you have to have stitches?"

One of Betsy's life goals was to have stitches.

"Yes, and a rabies shot," said Natalie.

"Natalie's telling us about the time she was bitten by a German shepherd," said Mum. "It has made her nervous of dogs."

62   Megan stared at Natalie and said nothing. It doesn't give her the right to kick them.

There was a silence and Natalie jumped in. "I see you're a Brownie, Betsy. I was a Brownie, too."

"You were?" Mum pounced on the remark like Bumper jumping on his rawhide bone. "Where did you meet?"

"Saint Jude's Church Hall."

"Then did you go on to Guides?" Mum asked hungrily.

"Yes," said Natalie, "the whole thing. Pathfinders, even Rangers. Are you a Pathfinder, Megan?"

"No. I don't like groups with uniforms. Too much like the army."

Mum gave Megan the look. But Natalie just laughed. "I know what you mean. My falling-out with Rangers happened when they wouldn't let me go on the peace march wearing my uniform. Too political, they said. So I quit in protest. But I did like it, especially for the friends."

"I guess that was really important for you, being an only child," said Mum.

"And the badges," said Betsy. "Did you get badges?"

"Some," said Natalie. "Mummy probably has them somewhere. She keeps everything, Popsicle-stick art, all that stuff."

Mummy? What kind of grown-up still calls their Mum "Mummy"? thought Megan.

Betsy tapped Natalie on the knee. "Hey! Do you know—" She began to sing:

"We are guides, all guides,
And in unexpected places,
You will meet our friendly faces,
And a helping hand besides. . . ."

Natalie joined in,

"And there's not much danger,
Of finding you're a stranger,
For Brownie, Guide, or Ranger,
We are guides, all guides."

Megan reached out and grabbed a huge handful of deluxe nuts. Mum wouldn't notice. She was hypnotized, hypnotized by the dog kicker.

Over dinner Natalie told them about a lecture on asteroids that she had attended the day before.

"You go to school on Saturdays?" asked Betsy.

"Not usually, but there was a visiting geophysicist giving a special lecture that I didn't want to miss. Asteroids aren't my field, but they are fascinating. This fellow has a theory that it was an asteroid whacking into the earth that caused the big land mass to break up into continents. Of course the geophysics mafia are resisting the theory like mad."

"What's a theory?" said Betsy.

"Sort of like a story about what might have happened."

"But is it true?"

"When it's proved, it's true. But until then it's a theory."

"How big are these asteroids?" asked Mum.

"Huge. The continent smasher one was probably about six miles across."

"What would happen if one landed on you?" said Betsy.

"Oh, you don't need to worry about that," said Natalie. "The chances are extremely rare. This all happened about two hundred fifty million years ago. Most of the bodies that enter the earth's atmosphere just burn up; that's what shooting stars are."

64   "But what would happen if one *did* land on you?" persisted Betsy.

"You would be well and truly squashed," said Natalie.

"Death by asteroid squashing," said Dad with relish. "That would be a good tragic end."

Natalie looked a bit surprised. Mum laughed. "I should explain, in case you think we're a family of weirdos. Jim and the girls are very fond of stories in which someone comes to an unusual end. It doesn't turn my crank, but they seem to love it."

"What kind of things?" asked Natalie.

"Oh, kidnapping by aliens, going through a car wash in a convertible and being vibra-shined, being recycled, that sort of thing," said Dad.

"Megan does a wonderful 'Sucked by a Leech,'" said Mum. "Come on, Megan."

No way. Megan shook her head. "I don't remember it."

There was a little pause. Megan didn't look at Mum.

"I think I do," said Dad.

"I'd love to hear it," said Natalie.

"Okay. Little Hortense, poor little Hortense, such a good child she was. She was kind to helpless animals and guppies. Never a cross word passed her lips. One day she was wading in the river, gathering watercress to make a nourishing soup for the poor, when she was attacked by leeches. Poor little Hortense, she was never a sturdy child to begin with, having given all her meals to stray dogs and birds, so before help could arrive, she was sucked dry, absolutely dry, like a beach ball before you blow it up."

Natalie was giggling. She caught on right away. "So, this asteroid, who does it squish?"

"Kevin," said Betsy. Her victims were always called Kevin.

"I thought Kevin was killed by a computer virus," said Dad.

"That was a different Kevin."

Natalie laid down her knife and fork. "So this Kevin is squashed by an asteroid, as flat as a pancake."

"Flatter," said Dad. "He is so thin he disappears if you turn him sideways."

"Two-dimensional," said Natalie, "no depth of character."

"Talks entirely in clichés," said Mum, "like 'today is the first day of the rest of your life.'"

Megan thought of Mr. Jessup, her soccer coach. "A team is only as strong as its weakest member." But she wasn't going to say it. How dare Dad tell Natalie the leech story? That was their story, not something to give away to strangers.

"What does 2-D Kevin think about art?" said Dad.

"He doesn't know much about it, but he knows what he likes," said Natalie. "Here's one—when 2-D Kevin loves something what does he do with it?"

"He lets it go," chorused Mum and Dad.

"Hang on," said Dad. "What does 2-D Kevin think about Christmas?"

Betsy had been following this conversation like someone at a tennis match, watching the ball move back and forth across the net in a long rally. She pounded on the table. "He thinks that it's really fun and he gets lots of presents!"

All the grown-ups laughed. Megan rolled her eyes. Betsy was so dumb. "That's not a cliché, Betsy. You don't get it at all."

Betsy's face began to crumple. Mum gave Megan the look again. I'm going to get it later, thought Megan, but not in front of a guest. A reckless feeling overtook her, as though she were wearing armor.

Now that she had blown it twice, it wasn't going to get any worse. From now on she could say anything she wanted.

Then Natalie reached over and covered Betsy's hand with her own. "That's exactly what I think about Christmas."

How obvious could you get? Megan took a big bite of salad and chewed loudly. Sucking up to everybody. Well, I'm not taken in. Talk about 2-D Kevin —what about a 2-D sister? A dog-abusing 2-D half sister?

CHAPTER TEN

Aᴛᴛᴇʀ ᴅɪɴɴᴇʀ ᴍᴜᴍ ᴅɪᴅ ᴀɴ ᴜɴʜᴇᴀʀᴅ-ᴏғ ᴛʜɪɴɢ ᴀɴᴅ left the dirty dishes on the table. Usually she was whipping them out from under you while you were still swallowing dessert. "Let's go into the living room for coffee, shall we?"

Natalie made some noises about helping with the dishes, but Mum said, "Oh, no, the dishwasher will do them." As though the dishwasher cleared the dishes and scraped and loaded itself, thought Megan. Natalie must know that as well as anyone. Lying again. Or was that a "convention," too? She tried to catch her co-dishwasher's eye, but Betsy was off on cloud nine somewhere.

There was more chat, during which Megan concentrated on eating as many after-dinner mints as possible. She looked at people's mouths talking and let her mind wander, until a change in Natalie's tone of voice caught her attention.

Natalie set down her coffee cup and sat up straighter. "So, I have a favor to ask you two girls. For my wedding in July—well, it's not going to be a big elaborate event, Franklin and I don't want that —but I would like . . . but I was wondering if you would be my flower girl and bridesmaid."

"Flower girl! Me?" Betsy flung herself backward onto the couch cushions. "Miranda was a flower girl and she got to wear lace gloves and nylons. Would I get to?"

"We'll see," said Mum.

Usually "we'll see" drove Betsy nuts, but instead she threw her arms around Natalie. "I've wanted to be a flower girl all my life."

Natalie smiled over Betsy's head. It *was* funny. Betsy had only heard about flower girls a few months before. Megan could have shared Natalie's look. But she didn't.

"How about you, Megan?" said Natalie.

"No, thank you. I would rather not." Megan smiled pleasantly at Natalie. She saw an abrupt movement from Mum out of the corner of her eye.

A shadow crossed Natalie's face, but she recovered. "I can understand that. It might be more fun for you at the wedding if you didn't have to be on show. Sometimes when I think of it, I wish I could come as a guest, too. But if you want to think about it a bit, Megan, that's fine, too."

"No, I've made up my mind. But thanks for asking me." Megan kept her voice bright and perky.

"How come you don't want to, Megan? It'll be fun." Betsy grinned.

"I would just prefer not to."

"Silly," said Betsy happily. "Do I get to wear a long dress?"

"If you like," said Natalie.

"Good. My feet would show even if I had a long dress, so I think I really should wear nylons. Do I get to?"

Megan glanced over at Natalie. How was Natalie going to handle this? Natalie didn't know how stubborn Betsy could be, or how she could lose it in a second. Natalie was looking at Mum in a "help me" sort of way. She raised her eyebrows and wrinkled up one corner of her mouth.

In that instant there was Mum, looking out of Natalie's face. That was just what Mum did, that pretzel mouth. That was the way she looked at Dad. Megan's armor fell off her with a clunk. It was true. Natalie was really Mum's *daughter*. Nothing would change that. It was like hearing the secret for the first time. She had known it in her head. Now she knew it in her stomach.

Natalie left soon after. Mum and Dad and Betsy seemed to want to stay in the living room and do an instant replay of the whole evening. Megan wandered away and let Bumper out of the basement. Then she began to clear up the dishes.

"Megan!" Mum called out to her. "You can be excused from that tonight."

"No, it's okay."

One more person sure made a lot more dishes. It was somehow important that they all fit in the dishwasher. Megan changed the places of large and small plates and managed to fit in two more cups.

Betsy came in and sat on the kitchen stool.

"Betsy!" Dad's voice floated in from the living room. "Are you on your way to brush your teeth?"

"Yes," said Betsy, sitting tight. She fed a little bit of chicken to Bumper. "I think Natalie's nice, don't you?"

"What's nice about her?"

"She smells nice."

"That's just because she wears perfume."

"Do you think Mum would let me wear perfume?"

"No chance." Megan reversed the order of the bowls. "Betsy?"

"Uh-huh."

"How come you're not more surprised?"

"About what?"

"About *Natalie*. About all of a sudden finding out that Mum has a grown-up child."

"Well, Granny does."

"Granny does what?"

"Granny has a grown-up child. That's Dad."

Megan threw a handful of cutlery into the cutlery container. It made a good loud crash. "Betsy! That's different. Oh, forget it, dumbball, you're hopeless."

"*I'm not a dumbball.*" Betsy spit out each word like a bullet. Her voice began to rise. "You're not allowed to call me a dumbball."

"So tell."

Betsy sat on the stool looking as if she would explode. She would never ever tattle.

Dad came into the kitchen and pretended to get mad when he saw Betsy. "What! Not in bed?" he roared, and came at Betsy as though to scoop her up. Betsy burst into tears and Dad stopped dead in his tracks. "Honey, what's the matter?"

"She's just overexcited," said Megan, not turning around from the dishes.

"*I am not overexcited.*" Betsy sure had a big voice for her size.

"Okay, okay," said Dad. "Come on, let's get ready for bed and see what Mr. Holmes is doing tonight." Betsy allowed herself to be led away, sobbing and hiccuping.

Megan tried to pour chicken grease from the roasting pan into a soup can without spilling. The door opened and Mum came in. She took the pan out of Megan's hands.

"Thanks for helping to clean up," said Mum.

"Hmmm," said Megan. It was escape, not helpfulness. She ran the dishcloth across the counter. Mum was probably about to bawl her out for being rude, or else she was going to ignore that and talk about Natalie. Either way Megan knew she wouldn't be able to stand it. If Mum said one word about Natalie, just one word, Megan knew she was going to do something very bad. Hurling the soup can of grease across the kitchen would feel really good.

"So . . ." said Mum.

Megan's hand edged toward the can.

"Ears healing up okay?"

What? "Um, yeah, they're fine."

"I must say, your earrings look great. It makes me half think — well, no, about one-sixteenth think — that I might take the plunge." Mum turned on the taps in the sink full blast. Steam and bubbles started to rise. "Maybe if I start thinking about it now, I might be ready in five years and I can go with Betsy."

Megan picked up a tea towel, but Mum took it out of her hands. "Leave this mess now. I'll finish up. You look beat."

Megan went downstairs and threw the tennis ball for Bumper. The mad part of her was still there. And now there was nowhere for it to go. Nowhere. Happily ever after. What a laugh. Mum must be unhappy about the bridesmaid thing. Wasn't she going to say anything? Was she just going to lie by silence again? The voice of Megan the fair interrupted. "But you didn't want her to say anything." Megan the mad threw the ball harder and harder. "Oh, shut up."

If there were some small but precise asteroids that could fall out of the sky and wipe out the events of the past two weeks, this would be the perfect moment.

CHAPTER ELEVEN

"So the queen, the mother of Princess Mayonnaise, was taken to the judge.

"'Have you ever lied to your children?' asked the judge.

"'No,' said the queen boldly.

"'Are you sure?' asked the judge again.

"The queen began to tremble.

"'Have you ever lied by leaving out things?' asked the judge sternly.

"'Yes,' admitted the prisoner.

"'Then you are banished to the forest,' said the judge. 'Woodcutter! Take this woman to the forest and bring me back her heart.'"

Megan blocked everything on the screen and deleted it, sending the words out into the ozone. Princess Mayonnaise and her keyboard of power.

But it wasn't getting her anywhere on daily life in the Stone Age, Mr. Mostyn's latest assignment. The encyclopedia didn't mention what Stone Agers ate for breakfast. Maybe Erin had some better books. Maybe she should go over there. Maybe she should just do nothing. She switched off the computer and turned on the TV.

Megan had taken to spending a lot of time at Erin's. The Hungerford house was just too full of Natalie. Not Natalie the person — she didn't visit very often—but Natalie the wedding. Mum had now met Natalie's mother, "Mummy," and they had decided to join forces on catering the wedding reception. "Mummy" was going to buy the ingredients and Mum would do the cooking. This plan seemed to involve long daily phone discussions. "Operation Matrimony," that's what Dad called it.

On TV three men hidden behind a screen were answering questions from a blond woman with large hair. "What is your idea of a romantic evening?"

Bumper wandered into the room. He had a tea towel wrapped around him. Betsy followed.

"Betsy, what are you doing?"

"I have a theory that Bumper is a horse. Do you have anything I could use as stirrups?"

Transformation was not a new experience for Bumper. Over the years Betsy had turned him into a movie star (sunglasses), an Hawaiian princess (a plastic lei), and a coffee table (no props required). Bumper was usually patient about these costumes, although he sometimes got a vagued-out look on his face, as in, "I am not here. This is not happening."

Bumper gave a sigh and flopped over on the floor.

"Oh, well." Betsy sat down beside Megan. On the screen Large Hair was about to make her choice. Would it be Brad, Chip, or Dirk for the dream date?

"Hey!" Betsy poked Megan.

"Shhhhhh."

Large Hair chose Dirk.

"Okay, what?"

"Would you rather spend ten days in jail or give Bumper away?"

"What?"

"If you *had* to choose."

Mum came downstairs, saving Megan from the decision. "That was Nat on the phone."

Nat, gnat. A little buzzing insect that flies around your head. On TV the studio audience roared their approval as Dirk kissed Large Hair.

"She wonders if we're free to go dress shopping next Saturday."

"For my flower girl dress?" said Betsy.

"Yes, and a new dress for Megan. I think this is a good excuse for us all to get dolled up."

"Yes!" said Betsy.

Since Mum had started school, she hadn't taken Megan downtown shopping once. Probably wouldn't be doing it now if it weren't for that gnat. But — a new dress. She hadn't expected that. "What about Art Experience?"

"We'll pick you up from the art school, then bus it downtown and hit those shops."

"Okay."

Betsy pulled the lace out of one of her shoes and tried to tie it around Bumper's head. He gave a whine and retreated under the chair. Old Paint had had enough.

The bus from the art school to downtown was crowded.

"What are hem-or-rhoids?" said Betsy in a loud voice.

People giggled. Megan clung to her pole and looked elsewhere. Life was more embarrassing since Betsy had learned to sound out.

"A medical condition," said Mum briskly. "Ring the bell, Betsy, our stop is coming up."

In the department store they escalatored up to the children's-wear floor.

"This is fun," said Natalie. "I love shopping, but Franklin is allergic to it."

"Does he get a rash?" asked Betsy.

"No, he just gets mournful if I make him go into stores. He's just not very interested in clothes or in possessions of any sort, really."

Betsy spied her dress on a model at the entrance to Rainbow Unicorn. It had green and cream stripes, with roses in the cream part. It had a big lace collar and lace around the cuffs. The fabric was soft and shiny.

"Now *that's* a party dress," said Mum.

A salesclerk appeared. "Lovely, isn't it? A dress for a little princess. They're on a rack right over here."

Oh, gack, thought Megan. She stared at the clerk, who wore a lot of makeup and was smiling, but only with her mouth.

"Let's see it on." The clerk had the dress off the hanger and all of them in the big fitting room before anyone could say a word. "Call me if you need me. That's going to look just charming."

Natalie looked at Megan and raised her eyebrows. Megan made a yucko face.

But the thing was, the dress did make Betsy look like a princess, a princess in a fairy-tale book.

"Just look at the buttons," said Mum. A row of rose-shaped buttons down the front of the dress exactly matched the roses in the fabric. "Turn around."

Betsy extended her arms and twirled around.

"The cream will match my dress," said Natalie.

Mum nodded. "Dare we look at the price?" She pulled out her glasses from her purse and looked at the ticket. She gulped. "Oh, my goodness."

Betsy held herself around the waist as though to keep the dress on by force. "It's a flower-girl dress," she said. "It has flowers."

"Oh, well," said Mum, "when you put it that way."

"Yea!" Betsy raised both arms like a prizefighter. "Thank you. Thank you. Thank you."

While Mum paid for the dress, Megan and Natalie wandered around the racks. The salesclerk descended on them. "Are we looking for something for you as well?" she asked, staring at Megan.

"No," said Megan.

"Yes," said Natalie.

The clerk heard the yes. She started whipping dresses up against Megan. Megan just wanted to escape.

"I don't think so. No, thanks."

"You just can't see the potential until you try it on."

By the time Mum returned with Betsy and a big shopping bag, the clerk was shepherding Megan and four dresses back into the changing room.

"We'll wait out here," said Mum.

Megan took her time pulling off her clothes. She looked at the dresses. It didn't matter which she tried on first. She hated them all. Try one and then get out of here. She was just pulling one over her head when the salesclerk burst in. "Need a little hand?"

"No," said Megan from inside the dress.

The clerk, who had very selective hearing, zipped the dress up the back. "Oh, that's very sweet. Let's show the others." She pushed Megan out the door.

Megan stood in front of the mirror. The dress made her look absolutely ridiculous, like some too-tall, bony Alice in Wonderland with stupid hair and a zit on her chin. She stood stiffly, trying not to let the dress touch her body. Her arms and legs looked as if they didn't belong to a human being, much less her. But the clerk didn't give her a chance to say anything. She was hovering, giving the dress little tucks, and poking Megan in the process, until Megan could hardly keep from hitting her.

"We'd like to take a little dart here, and of course you don't quite get the effect with runners." The clerk gave a revolting little laugh.

Megan looked down at the growths at the end of her legs.

"Perhaps you'd like to try one of the other styles."

The worst thing was that Megan could see how beautiful the dress was, how beautiful it would have looked on her when she was Betsy's age. But now it made her feel like a mutant.

"A size larger?" asked the salesclerk.

"No." Natalie's voice was clear and definite. "The size is not the problem. That dress is just far too young for Megan. We're in the wrong department."

"Ah," said the salesclerk, "thinking of a more sophisticated image, were we?" She gave Natalie that making-fun-of-kids-while-pretending-to-be-nice look.

Natalie didn't play along. "We'll be fine on our own now, thank you."

Megan fled to the change room and put her normal human being clothes back on again. But even in them she felt misshapen, as though the dress had warped her. She couldn't even imagine something that she could wear to a wedding. And she sure wasn't in the mood for more shopping.

She emerged from the change room. "Can I just wear my blue dress from last summer?"

Mum looked disappointed. "Sure, if you like. Don't you want to look at some other things, though? Nat has some ideas about other shops we could try."

Megan just shook her head. Mum's disappointed voice made her itchy with irritation. Hadn't she just saved Mum a whole bunch of money? Mum should be grateful, not sad-sounding. Oh, why was everything she did *wrong*? Maybe she really was as mutant as she felt in that dress. Going shopping used to be fun. Now everything was just . . . impossible.

When Megan went to bed that night Betsy's dress was hanging in the window. She went to lift it down.

"Don't."

Great. Betsy was still awake. "But I can't close the curtains."

"We don't need to."

"But people can see in."

"Not with the dress hanging there. I need to have it there."

Betsy was becoming a real whiner. "Oh, all right."

"Megan, I have a theory that Princess Mayonnaise is going to get married."

"Why am I not surprised?"

"What?"

"Nothing. Betsy, you've already handed in your story. You beat Kevin Blandings. Why are you still making up things about Mayonnaise?"

"I just like to think about her. She's going to have five bridesmaids and one flower girl. The flower girl gets to wear nylons, lipstick, perfume, and nail polish."

"I didn't even know she had a boyfriend. Who's she marrying?"

"I haven't made up that part yet. A prince."

"I thought she was going to be a superhero."

"She still is, but I'm not thinking about that. The flower girl carries a big bunch of tulips and daffodils and those white ones with pink middles."

"Does she drop them?"

"No, of course not."

"Does she come first down the aisle?"

Betsy paused. "Does she?"

"Yes, and everybody stares at her. She can't make any mistakes."

"Well, she doesn't."

"No? She doesn't have to go to the bathroom in the middle of the wedding? But she can't leave so she pees her pants?"

"No! That's not what happens."

Megan laughed. "And the whole wedding has to be called off and the prince sent home?"

"Shut up!"

"Okay, okay, just kidding. What really happens?"

Betsy did not reply.

"Come on, tell me the rest of the story."

"I don't want to."

"Sheesh, can't even take a joke. Forget it, then." Megan patted the edge of her bed and Bumper, with a woof of delight, jumped up beside her.

"Hey! You're not allowed to have Bumper on the bed."

"So tell." Megan put her cassette headphones over her ears and turned up the volume loud. Streetlight seeped in along the sides of the dress in the window and fell on Betsy's shelf of stuffed animals. Their staring eyes glowed. Megan turned to the wall. This room was too crowded. This house was too crowded. This family was too crowded. In her mind she pushed her canoe off from shore and paddled straight ahead toward the line where the ocean falls off the edge of the world.

CHAPTER TWELVE

"IF SHE'S COMING, I'M NOT COMING."

Megan sat on an overturned bucket in the garage. Dad was kneeling on the floor, painting an eagle onto the side of a huge box kite.

"But you have to come," said Dad. "It's Kite Day. I'll need your help. Betsy's too short and Mum doesn't concentrate."

"But why is Natalie coming?"

Dad squinted as he painted a small yellow dot in the eagle's eye. "Perfect. There's a raptor if I ever saw one." He blew on the eagle eye. "Don't you think you might get to like Natalie if you knew her a bit better?"

Megan picked at the scab on her knee. "No."

"She's coming because it's our chance to meet Franklin the fiancé, apparently."

"I don't care."

"What I'm hoping," said Dad, "is that some kind of brave eagle spirit will get into this kite and save it from . . ."

"Crashing?" said Megan.

"Yeah," said Dad. "There is nothing more depressing than winding up the string of a kite that has committed suicide. Not to mention embarrassing."

"Well, you should know."

Dad flicked his paintbrush at Megan. "Brat face. I realize I had a slight problem last year."

"And the year before that."

"But that was the year it rained. According to the weather station the percentage possibility of precipitation for Saturday is zero. This is my year for triumph. I can feel it in my bones."

"You mean this is your year to be dynamic and innovative?" said Megan.

Dad snorted. "You are a wicked, cruel child." He held up the kite and turned it slowly. "So, what about it? Will you come?"

It was a big park. There would be lots of room to escape. "Okay."

The percentage possibility of precipitation remained at zero and Kite Day dawned with sunny skies. A gentle but steady wind blew in off the sea. The park was busy with strolling clowns and musicians, a balloon sculptor, joking jugglers, and a huge blue sky full of kites.

Betsy made a friend, and they found a piece of wood and spent their time floating it back and forth across the pond. Franklin was arriving at suppertime, and Mum and Natalie sat on the blanket and talked. Why bother coming? thought Megan. She and Dad took part in the Great Kite Fly-By and then lay on the grass and watched the fighting kites battle it out. Prizes were awarded to the biggest, smallest, and most beautiful kites, and to the oldest and youngest fliers. The eagle didn't win a prize, but it didn't crash either. Dad launched it for a final flight.

"Want a turn?" he said, handing the reel to Megan. "I'm going to take a break and see how everyone is doing. It looks like they're in that face-painting lineup." He pointed toward a long, meandering line of people.

Megan held the reel high and let the kite pull her, gently but definitely, toward the beach. She played out the string until the pressure slackened, but not too much. She stopped in the middle of the field. All around her other kite fliers were standing or slowly walking, all with the same look of concentration. She guided the eagle through a big figure 8.

At the far end of the field, near the marina, there were a couple of remote-control planes flying tight circles in the air. The snarl of their engines started to bug Megan. She had tried it once and it had been fun for a while, and then boring. The plane just went wherever you made it go. She stared up at the eagle kite. You can make a kite do what you want, but not always. If you're too bossy, it just crashes. But if you get it right, it is as though a little bit of you goes out your fingers and up the string and gets to be where the kite is, high and free.

She turned around and looked back toward the face-painting tent. The line was shorter. Time to go back. She carefully reeled in the kite and strolled back to the others.

"He said he would be here at five," said Natalie. "There aren't two face-painting tents, are there?"

"I don't think so," said Mum. "Anyway, if Franklin is a bit late, it's just as well, considering how slowly this line is moving."

"Yes," said Natalie, "this hasn't been very well planned. You'd think they would have more face painters at peak times. Or some system whereby you could take a number or book a time in advance. It wouldn't be that hard to organize."

"I don't know," said Dad. "I find it a bit of a relief doing something that doesn't involve an appointment. So much of life is scheduled."

Natalie looked earnestly at Dad. "But poor organization just erodes time and causes frustration."

Dad shrugged. "You're probably right."

He turned to Megan. "So, a crash-free day so far, kiddo. What do you think? Shall we quit while we're ahead?"

Megan handed the kite to Dad and then sat on the ground and leaned back against her elbows. A yellow sun kite floated overhead, drawing big slow circles on the blue. Bright fighting kites whipped and snapped and scribbled around it. An airplane trailing a banner that said KEEP FIT AT ARNIE'S GYM buzzed behind it all.

Betsy was in a panic of choice. As each painted face emerged she changed her mind.

"I think I'll have a unicorn."

"No, maybe a rainbow and stars."

"Oh, look, a dog face."

"Maybe polka dots are better."

She was bouncing from foot to foot, with a new idea on each bounce.

"Hope this face painter is the decisive type," said Dad as Betsy went into the tent.

She must have been, because Betsy came out minutes later with a wide grin and the bottom half of her face painted like a big piece of watermelon. After the first round of admiration Natalie said, "There he is. Franklin! Over here!"

A tall, thin man with a beard loped over the field toward them. When he was introduced he shook everyone's hand, including Megan's and Betsy's. He didn't do it as though he were being cute.

Mum laid claim to a table by the duckpond and started unpacking the picnic. Covered bowls, plastic bags, thermoses, bottles. It was like a pile of presents. By the time everyone was crowded in at the table, with rearrangements of left- and right-handed people to avoid fork collisions, Megan was starving. She purloined a roll to tide her over until the dishes were properly passed.

"Potato salad, Franklin?" said Mum.

"No, thank you," said Franklin. "I don't," pause, "eat eggs."

Franklin was a slow talker; well, not exactly slow, but he left gaps.

"Oh, too bad," said Mum, passing a thermos. "Mushroom soup?"

"Soup on a picnic?" said Betsy.

"Remember last year?" said Mum. "We were all so cold."

"Does this have a . . . meat base?" asked Franklin, holding the thermos frozen in the air.

"Yes, chicken stock. Oh, Franklin, I'm sorry. Natalie told us you were a vegetarian, but I forgot about chicken stock. Tell you what, there's lots of salad and stuff. Why don't you just help yourself?"

"That would probably be the . . . best approach," said Franklin.

That little pause that Franklin put into the middle of sentences, thought Megan, was always the same length. Like three beats in music.

Betsy turned to Franklin, who was sitting beside her. "Are you a picky eater?"

"Betsy!" said Mum.

"No, that's a legitimate question," said Franklin. "If you mean do I pick my food carefully," beat, beat, beat, "then you could say that I am."

"Goody," said Betsy. "I'm a picky eater, too. But I never met a grown-up who was one."

Mum looked embarrassed and gave a little laugh, but Franklin just gave Betsy a slow, serious nod and went back to peeling an apple.

"So, Franklin," said Dad, "where are you from?"

Franklin put down the apple. "Many places, really. Where are we all from?"

Dad looked confused.

"Franklin's family moved a lot," piped up Natalie.

Dad looked confident again. "Oh yes, military family, were you?"

"No, not military." Megan beat three beats on her celery stick. "Just peripatetic."

Megan stared at Franklin's beard. It was very dark brown but thin. You could see his chin through it. It moved up and down with each chew. She felt her fingers making a pair of scissors to cut it off and make his face tidy. You could also see, under his mustache, that his lips were sort of wet-looking. What would it be like to kiss Franklin? You'd get that mustache in your mouth. Yuck. But Natalie must like it. Funny that somebody as pretty as Natalie . . . Megan caught herself. Oh, all right — she crunched down hard on her celery—Natalie was pretty. Anyway, she didn't seem to match with Franklin, who was sort of odd-looking.

Between rounds of food (what would pasta salad and potato chips be like as a sandwich filling in a bun? A spirit of scientific inquiry demanded that she try it) Megan spied on Natalie to see how a person about to be married looked. Apart from staring at Franklin and reaching over to take a piece of leaf out of his hair, Natalie acted fairly normal. Where was all that running toward each other in slow motion through a field of wildflowers stuff? Maybe that was for private. Or maybe that was for shampoo commercials. Did real older sisters talk about all that with real younger sisters?

Natalie had an evening lecture, so she and Franklin left right after chocolate cake. As they were standing up, Dad gave Franklin a big arm-pumping handshake. "Real good to meet you."

Megan watched them walk across the field toward the parking lot. They weren't even holding hands. No shampoo ad there.

"Gosh," said Dad, "Franklin's pretty heavy going."

"He's a serious young man," said Mum. "Obviously thinks deeply about things."

"And what did he say about his family? I couldn't catch it. Epileptic or something?"

"Peripatetic." Mum was burping Tupperware in an impatient way. "Means moves around a lot."

"Doesn't he seem like a bit of a stick to you? A bit dull for Natalie?"

"Not at all. I think she's very proud of him. Apparently he's a brilliant young geophysicist." Mum's face started to get that dried Play-Doh look.

"That's it, then," said Dad. He grabbed the last piece of cake before Mum could wrap it up. "He spends too much time with rocks. He's slowed down to their pace. Rocks don't exactly live in the fast lane." He grinned.

Mum did not. "I don't think geophysicists spend that much time with rocks. They examine theoretical questions about the origin of the earth."

Dad nodded his head, pretending to be serious. "Oh."

Mum continued. "And she is almost a PhD, after all. You wouldn't expect her to be engaged to some used-car salesman or something."

Dad raised his eyebrows. "Or some hack writer with half a B.A. I guess."

Mum threw a handful of cutlery into the picnic basket. "Did I say anything about writers?"

"Okay, okay. But come off it, Judy. Didn't you find him a bit pompous?"

"No, I didn't."

Lying, thought Megan. Lying again.

"All right," said Dad. "Difference of opinion. I'm going to pack up the kite."

In the car on the way home there was an extra passenger, an argument. Megan hated that unexploded feeling when two people are fighting and pretending that they aren't. Dad tapped on the steering wheel and Mum stared out the window. Betsy sat hunched in her corner and picked her fingernails. She hadn't done that since the first week of second grade. Megan reached over and covered her hand.

Betsy pulled away and sat up straight. "Rocks do, too, live in the fast lane," she said.

"What?" said Mum.

"Rocks do live in the fast lane. Remember that rock that fell off that rock truck and bounced down the road and broke the window in our car when we went camping at that lake with the million mosquitoes?"

Dad snorted and Mum's shoulders lost their frozen look.

"Good point," said Dad.

"Anyway, I *like* Franklin," said Betsy.

"Good for you," said Dad.

"Oh well, you like *everyone*," said Megan.

Betsy bounced on the seat. "Do not."

"I *was* a little defensive with that hack writer remark," said Dad.

Mum turned to him. "Am I sometimes a pain in the neck about Natalie?"

Always, always, thought Megan.

"Sometimes," said Dad, "a bit obsessed."

Mum got pretzel mouth. "Sorry."

"Ditto," said Dad.

The extra passenger got sucked out the open window.

"I do *not* like everyone," said Betsy. "I don't like Kevin Blandings. I don't like the rat in *Charlotte's Web*. I don't like that mean lady in the school store. I don't like Herod. I don't like . . ."

"Okay, okay, okay. I take it back." Megan sighed. Sometimes with Betsy you had to lose in order to win.

CHAPTER THIRTEEN

THERE WERE STILL THREE WEEKS UNTIL THE WEDDING, and already it had thoroughly invaded the house. The kitchen was action central, as catering plans geared up to full swing. Wonderful food kept appearing, only to disappear hours later into the freezer. Little meatballs and tiny quiches, walnut squares and pans of brownies. Now you see them, now you don't.

"There's never been so much good food in the house," said Dad mournfully, "and we aren't allowed to eat any of it."

And Mum's conversations were bizarre. "How many celery sticks would you eat at a buffet lunch?"

"If they have cheese in them, I would eat ten," said Betsy.

"None," said Dad. "You get those long strings in your teeth, and if you don't have your dental floss—and who's going to bring dental floss to a wedding?—then you spend your whole time trying to suck the celery strings out from between your teeth, without looking like you're doing it."

Megan didn't offer an opinion. Mum didn't notice.

Then there was the business about the Gift. Natalie and Franklin wanted a tent for a wedding present. So outdoor equipment catalogs began appearing, with complicated descriptions of aluminum alloy poles and geodesic construction.

"This yellow one is jolly," said Dad.

"No," said Mum. "It has to be dark green. Natalie

says that bright colors on tents are a form of visual environmental pollution."

"Come off it," said Dad. "What about dandelions and, oh I don't know, yellow birds. Are they environmental pollution?"

"Well, don't ask me," said Mum. "She just feels very strongly about this."

"Oh well, if Natalie has spoken." Dad rolled his eyes and retreated to the garage. The garage had never been so neat. Even the nails were sorted.

Megan's retreat was her room, and she felt, as she closed the door, like someone in a medieval castle pulling up the drawbridge. But that wedding-free zone didn't last. One day Megan found Betsy sitting on the bedroom floor taking coins out of her fuzzy-dog purse and piling them up into towers.

"What are you doing?" asked Megan.

"I need four hundred more cents."

"So, save your allowance for four weeks."

"But four weeks is after the wedding, isn't it?"

"Is this another wedding-present idea? You know, we're included in the tent thing. We don't have to get Natalie a present on our own."

Betsy pulled a torn, creased piece of paper from her pocket and spread it out on the carpet. "But I want to. Isn't this beautiful?"

A full-page glossy photo showed a big hunk of glass, carved to look like waves. Attached to the top was a silver killer whale, jumping: "The Monarch of the Deep."

"Where did you get this?"

"From a magazine. And look, it's got one of those send-away things. Like when Mum sent away for rubber stamps with our names on them. And I only need four hundred more cents."

Megan looked at the clipping again. "An heirloom in the making. Only $15.95." Funny, it looked like a pretty jazzy thing to get for $15.95. It must be made of cheap plastic or something. Then she noticed the asterisk.

"Betsy, it's not $15.95. It's $15.95 a month."

"What do you mean, 'a month'?"

"It means you have to pay $15.95 every month for a whole year. It really costs"—Megan grabbed a pencil and scribbled on a corner of the picture—"$191.40."

Betsy snatched back the clipping. "It does not. Look, $15.95. Right on top of the whale."

"See that star?" said Megan. "That means small print. You have to watch out for the small print."

"How many weeks' allowance is one hundred, what you said?"

"Too many," said Megan, standing up. "Sorry, kiddo." She went to the door. When she glanced back, Betsy had her head down on the table and was toppling her piles of coins, one by one. Megan paused. Maybe she should take Betsy down to the hardware store, where you could buy a present for ten dollars. But that would take all morning. Besides, it wasn't her fault. It was all this wedding thing. Practically making people buy you presents. Phony baloney.

It was a relief to go to school. Two more weeks and nobody was taking anything seriously. Mr. Mostyn spent his time telling them stories about how he worked on the fish boats rather than warning them about how the ax was going to fall when they got to junior high school next year if they didn't pull up their socks now. He brought in his tape deck and played music in the afternoons. There was a lazy, winding-down feeling in the air.

The librarian asked for volunteers to help mend textbooks, and Megan and Erin spent long afternoons in the library with glue and tape. Often they stayed long after the bell. The librarian brought them Cokes. They looked at the first-grade readers and remembered Jason and his happy dog, Bud. They talked about seventh grade.

"What do you think is going to be the best thing?" asked Erin.

"I don't know. Maybe lockers and electives."

"Wrong," said Erin. "Cafeteria and dissection."

"Are you sure we get to dissect in seventh grade?"

"Well, I sure hope so. Otherwise, what's the point?" Erin stood up and stretched and went to the sink to wash library paste off her hands. "Hey, there's some kid on the lookout tower in the playground sitting under an umbrella, and it's not even raining."

"Let's see." Megan went to the window. "That's an orange dinosaur umbrella just like Betsy's. Hold it, I think that *is* Betsy. She should have gone home half an hour ago. What's she doing? I better go see."

Megan crunched across the gravel of the playground. Yes, it was Betsy. There were her yellow sneakers sticking out from under her Dinosaur Museum umbrella. Megan rested her chin on the floor of the lookout and then reached through the railings and tipped the umbrella up.

Betsy's face was blotchy with tears, and her nose was running. "Go away."

Megan searched through her pockets for a Kleenex. No luck. "Betsy? What's wrong? Are you in trouble?"

A sob hiccuped out from behind the umbrella.

"Come on, I'll walk you home."

The umbrella tilted back. "I don't want to walk with you."

"Well, you can't stay here."

"Can, too." Betsy reached out and grabbed the railing.

"Betsy. Don't be a dumbball. You're so stubborn." Megan tried to pry Betsy's fingers off the bars.

Betsy roared: "Get away from me. I hate you I hate you I hate you."

"Oh, all *right*. Stay here, see if I care."

Megan stamped off. At the edge of the playground she turned back. Betsy was hidden under the umbrella again. She really shouldn't be left alone. Oh, forget it. She knew the rules about coming home. It wasn't Megan's fault if she was being difficult.

Mum was supervising a large boiling pot when Megan walked into the kitchen.

"Betsy's on the lookout tower at school and she won't come home."

"Why didn't you bring her?"

"Because *she wouldn't come*. She's really getting to be a brat."

"Okay, okay. Look, watch these eggs. When the timer dings, drain them and then put them into the bathtub right away."

"The bathtub?"

"It's the only way to cool three dozen eggs quickly enough. There's ice water in there. I'll go get Betsy."

Mum arrived home ten minutes later with a sobbing, hiccuping Betsy in tow.

She sat her on a chair and gave her a glass of water. "Now, what's wrong?"

"I got a *note*. From Mrs. Kozol. All during first grade I never got a note and this year I never got a note and now I got a note." Betsy's voice ended in a wail as she pulled an envelope out of her pocket.

"It's probably just some year-end party or something," said Megan. "What's the prob?"

"That's a *notice*," said Betsy furiously. "This is a *note*."

"Let's have a look," said Mum, slitting open the envelope. She pulled out a piece of paper and unfolded it. As she read she got a funny twitching around her mouth. She coughed. "So, Betsy, it seems as if Kevin Blandings's parents are a bit upset."

"Tattletale. Anyway, I gave him back his crummy five dollars."

Mum arranged her mouth again. "Mrs. Kozol says that you were trying to sell Kevin a lottery ticket. Is that right?"

Betsy nodded.

Megan grinned. "Where the heck did you get a lottery ticket?"

Betsy glared. "None of your beeswax."

"Megan, we don't need to hear from you. But, Betsy honey, where *did* you get a lottery ticket?"

Betsy looked out from under her eyebrows. "I just made it, with my junior printer. I made lots, but only Kevin Blandings would buy one, because he was the only one with five dollars. He keeps it in this little pocket in his shoe. He showed me. It's his emergency money."

Megan stared at Betsy. Not bad. As a money-making scheme it sure beat collecting pop bottles. There was one problem, though. "But if you only sold one ticket, then Kevin Blandings would win for sure, and you wouldn't make any money."

"He would *not*. Nobody ever wins the lottery. Dad says. When we go to the corner store and he buys one of those tickets he always says, 'I don't know why I bother. Nobody ever wins the lottery.'"

Megan snorted. "But, Betsy, that doesn't mean that nobody actually . . ."

Mum jumped in. "Megan, we know that you know. Put a lid on it. Oh rats, there's the phone. Can you get it? No, not in here. Get it in the living room."

Megan jogged into the next room, closing the door behind her. She flopped onto the couch. Maybe it was Erin.

"Hello. Is this Megan? This is Natalie."

"Oh, hi, Natalie. I'll get Mum."

"No, hang on. It's you I want to talk to."

"Yes?" No, I still don't want to be a brides-maid.

"I just wondered if you would like to come out to the university with me tonight to look through the telescope. It's a nice clear night and we'll have the place to ourselves."

Alone with Natalie? "Um, I don't know."

"The only thing is, and I need your advice on this, can I get away with not inviting Betsy? I don't want to leave her out, but she really is too young."

Megan heard the rising tones of Betsy in the kitchen. She was approaching blastoff. Escape was an attractive idea. Besides, to look at real stars, not fake ones at the planetarium—that would be fun.

"No, that's okay. Betsy doesn't need to come. But I'd like to. Wait a minute and I'll ask."

Back in the kitchen Mum was leaning against the counter, holding the note and hooting with laughter.

"Where's Betsy?"

"She went out to play. You know her powers of recovery. Thank goodness. I thought I was going to die if I had to be the responsible, serious parent for one more second. You know when you have to laugh but you're not allowed to?"

"Mum, can I go with Natalie to the telescope at the university tonight? She'll pick me up."

"What?" Mum dried her eyes on a tea towel. "Okay. Sounds like fun. I'll be bowling with Marie as usual. Dad and Betsy can stay home and think up some illegal scam." She exploded in another snort of laughter. "I do like this Mrs. Kozol. She thinks that Betsy has a bright future in the new economy of self-reliance and will leave the Kevin Blandings of this world behind in the dust. She's probably got a point. If only we can keep Betsy on the right side of the law."

CHAPTER FOURTEEN

THE CAMPUS WAS VERY QUIET AS NATALIE AND MEGAN walked from the parking lot. "Crazed astronomers are the only ones out here on a Friday night," said Natalie.

The observatory was small, dominated by the mysterious looming telescope. Natalie pressed a switch and a panel in the domed roof slid open, exposing a rectangle of night sky. She sat down at a computer terminal and blipped a bit.

"So, what would you like to see?"

"The moon, but it's not in that part of the sky."

Natalie grinned. "No problem." She pressed another switch and with a sliding sound the dome began to turn until the moon was framed perfectly. "The moon is a good choice for tonight. First quarter is good for shadows, you can really see things." She typed at the terminal and the telescope turned. "Okay, have a look."

Megan slid into position. The moon filled her vision. Light grey, like plasticine. Clear, with a sharp edge of darkness, and huge. Two smooth areas against a rougher area, and little pockmarks dotted over it.

"The top blob is the Sea of Tranquility," said Natalie, "and the one below is the Sea of Nectar. Not really seas, of course—plains."

"Fancy names," said Megan, holding one eye shut with her hand.

"Yes, I like them. The features of the moon were named three hundred years ago, and they went in for more romantic names than we do nowadays. The Lake of Dreams, the Bay of Rainbows."

"What are those pimple things?"

"Craters. Probably the result of asteroid collisions. See the one with the bright dot in the middle?"

"Yeah."

"That's Theophilus, sixty-seven miles wide, one of the biggies. The dot is a mountain at its center, catching the light."

"Wow." Megan stared. What did it remind her of? Oh, yeah, drops of water from the canoe paddle. But these things were miles wide. It would take days to walk across them. She tried to imagine walking on the moon. "It's hard to believe that it really is the moon and not, you know, made up. Do you spend a lot of time here?"

Natalie looked through the second eyepiece. "Yup, and in the winter it gets really cold. Sometimes I seem to spend all my time twiddling with the computer. But other times I don't work at all. I just stare. I like the flip that my mind does when I realize that I'm not looking out into space but back into time."

"Back? I don't get it."

"Do you know about light-years?"

Megan shook her head.

"Well, distances in space are so huge that we use light-years as a measure. A light-year is how far light travels in a year, about six million million miles."

"Wow, but how does that mean we're looking back in time?"

"Well, if a star is ten light-years away then we are seeing it as it was ten years ago."

Megan's brain started to hurt. "But we're still seeing it right now."

"Right now here, but not there. I had a professor who used to say that looking out into space is looking elsewhen rather than elsewhere. The stars we're seeing may not even exist anymore."

"What a rip-off!"

Natalie laughed. "I never thought of it that way. I guess I'm just used to living in two times."

"Find me one of those light-year stars."

"Okay." Natalie typed away at the computer for a minute, and the telescope moved above them in the darkness. "Here's Vega, twenty-seven light-years away. Fifty-eight times brighter than our sun."

Megan looked and looked, trying to believe that she was looking into the past. She started to feel as though she were floating, with nothing to hold onto. Something in her got big. She was falling into space, evaporating, going fuzzy at the edges. She caught herself grabbing onto the chair.

Natalie was talking. "It's all there. The whole history of the universe, written in the sky."

Megan thought of the asterisk leading to the small print, the truth. A message from each star.

Natalie continued: "All that information and we've only figured out how to read the tiniest bit of it."

It sounded as if Natalie were talking to herself. It was very relaxing.

"Megan, can I ask you something?"

Uh-oh. End of things being relaxed. Was this telescope thing just going to be an excuse for some revolting sister-to-sister talk? Was this question going to be, How come you've been acting like such a brat?

"Okay."

"What can you smell at the moment?"

Megan pulled her eyes away from the telescope. "Smell?"

"Yes, right at the moment. If you concentrate on all the things you can smell, what are they?"

Megan closed her eyes and inhaled. "Nothing. Air."

"Hmmm."

"Why?"

Natalie laughed. "Because I have this ridiculously strong sense of smell. If I could see like I can smell, I would have eyes like this telescope. And I've always wondered if it's something I inherited. I asked Judy, but she says her sense of smell is just normal. And I figured if Betsy had an extraordinary sense of smell, we'd all know about it. So I just wondered about you."

Wondering.

Dad looking in the mirror. "Glad you got my curly hair, Megan, as I have less of it every year."

The way Mum and Aunt Marie both had stick-out ears.

Mum standing back to back with John. "You're growing into a real beanpole, just like your dad."

Natalie didn't have any of this. Was she sad about it? Megan put her eye back to the telescope and tried to choose a safe way for the conversation to go. "So what can you smell at the moment?"

"Floor cleaner, the plastic smell of this equipment, and a whiff of Mike Swanson's aftershave. He must have been here earlier this evening. How come men don't realize that aftershave is completely unacceptable."

"Plastic doesn't smell."

"That's just what I mean. It does to me. I don't go around telling everyone this, though, because it makes them self-conscious. Like, everybody has this secret fear that they smell bad."

"Everyone?"

"I figure. Whenever I see—oh, I don't know, politicians, blabbing on and on about something like they know it all—I find it very comforting to know that in some part of their minds they're worried about their armpits."

Megan snorted. "They could hire you to tell them if they were okay."

Natalie grinned. "Good idea. That's a career opportunity I hadn't contemplated. If astronomy doesn't work out, I'll think about it. So, have you had enough for one night?"

"I think so."

"Okay. Next time we'll find some planets, the next-door guys."

Next time. So Natalie was going to invite her again? Megan felt suddenly shy and put her eye to the telescope for one last look at Vega. Everything had already happened on Vega. But on planet Earth there was still next time.

Natalie typed briskly on the computer. "Let me put things to bed here and we can go make hot chocolate in my office. It drives the janitor nuts when we make hot chocolate in there. One of a number of things that drive him nuts. We call him Dismal Seepage."

The panel slid shut and the night sky disappeared. Natalie turned on a light. The here and now crowded in.

CHAPTER FIFTEEN

WHEN MEGAN GOT HOME FROM THE UNIVERSITY MUM and Dad were in the kitchen. Dad was massaging Mum's shoulder and singing along to the radio. Some violin was sliding all over the place. Bumper was in the basement doorway impersonating a rug.

"So here's the stargazer," said Dad. "Did you see all those dippers and crabs and things?"

"No," said Megan, "we mostly looked at the moon."

"I never could see those constellations. Orion's belt and all that. In the books they put lines between the stars like dot-to-dot, but when you look up into the real sky, it always just looks like a bunch of stars to me."

"That's because you have a literal mind and no soul," said Mum. "Ow, that hurts."

"Good," said Dad. "That means we're hitting the spot. Bowler's shoulder. But listen, how can you accuse a man whose whole being vibrates to the sound of Stephane Grapelli of having no soul?"

Mum rolled her eyes. "So, did you have a good time?"

Megan nodded. "It was fun." How could she talk about elsewhen and the Bay of Rainbows in that bright, loud kitchen?

"A little to the left," said Mum, "aah."

"There's a computer in the room with the tele-scope," said Megan. "Natalie spends a lot of time doing that."

"Yup," said Dad, "I imagine that old Natalie has the universe pretty much recorded and under control."

"Jim . . ." Mum was using her warning but kidding voice.

The telephone rang and Dad held up his hand. "Listen! The phone's in the same key as the music. Okay, okay, I'm getting it. Oh, hi, Marie. Yes, she's right here." Dad put the receiver against Mum's ear and started to rub her back again.

Megan opened the dog-biscuit cupboard and Bumper rose from the dead, turned his head to one side, and whimpered. "Okay, boy." Megan tossed a biscuit bone into the air, and Bumper watched it fall safely to the floor before retrieving it. He didn't like his food on the wing. Megan scratched him behind the ears while he crunched.

"Wait a minute. I'll ask her." Mum balanced the phone on her shoulder. "Megan, when Marie got home there was a message from Mr. Thompson on the island. One of the windows of the cottage has been broken. He thinks it was a bird. So Marie and John are going to go over tomorrow to sort it out and then stay overnight. They'd like to take you and Betsy. Want to go?"

"Um, I don't know. I've got Art Experience."

"John's going to skip this week. But it's up to you."

Megan thought about escaping Operation Matrimony. "Sure."

"Hang on," said Dad. "Why don't you both go?"

"Impossible," said Mum. "Marie already suggested that, but I have far too much to do."

"Like what?" asked Dad.

"Like a turkey to cook," said Mum impatiently. "For turkey divan for the wedding."

"I'll do it," said Dad.

"You'll what? Yes, I'm still here, Marie. Jim's babbling."

"I don't have much on tomorrow. I'll barbecue it. Give me the phone for a minute. Hey, Marie, have you got Howie there? Can I speak to him please?"

Dad held the phone away from his ear. "You need a break, Judy. Look, your shoulders are heading up toward your ears just talking about the wedding. Howie? Feel like coming over tomorrow to watch the game and barbecue a turkey? Sure. Great. See you around ten." Dad handed the phone back to Mum. "There, all set."

Mum looked a bit dazed. "Well, I guess I'm coming, too, Marie. Early ferry? Okay. Thanks."

Mum hung up the phone. "Do you really know how to barbecue a turkey?"

"I've done chickens. Must be the same poultry principle. Don't worry. It'll be great. Scout's honor."

"You were never a scout."

"Picky, picky."

Bumper padded up the stairs with Megan and did a brief snuffle around the bedroom. But his heart wasn't in being awake and he settled back into dog dreams before Megan had even taken off her shoes.

The streetlight shone through the window onto the sleeping Betsy. She was scrunched up with her knees bent under her and her face smashed into the pillow. She looked like a turtle.

Megan went to the window to close the curtains. Only one star was visible beyond the bright streetlight. Only one sun. She leaned out the window into the cool breeze and sent her mind toward the star. She said the words "as fast as light," trying for that dizzy, dissolving feeling again. But it didn't work. She stayed right inside herself, like peanut butter in a jar.

And the star stayed right in the top branches of the chestnut tree across the street.

She pulled the curtain across the streetlight and the invisible sea of stars. She undressed in the dark and slid under the covers. She looked over to the turtle. Betsy was smaller when she was asleep.

Some time later Megan woke up to the sound of a dresser drawer opening. She peered into the darkness of the room. Betsy was scrabbling in the dresser, making a little hiccuping, crying sound. Megan glanced at the clock: 1:27.

"Betsy, what are you doing?"

"Mum didn't put my clothes out." Betsy sobbed and scooped out a handful of socks.

"But tomorrow's not a school day. You can choose your own clothes in the morning."

"I can't." There was a small scrabbling noise. Betsy sorted through the socks.

Megan's body was as heavy as wood, a tree rooted to the mattress. So warm, so sleepy . . .

The closet door squeaked open and Megan heard the sounds of hangers scraping across the rod. Betsy couldn't reach that high.

"Betsy, I'll help you in the morning."

"You won't."

Megan reached over and switched on her light. "Bets?"

Betsy turned her blotchy face to Megan. "I can't see what to get."

"Hey, guess what?"

"I don't want to guess."

"We're going to the island tomorrow."

"We are?"

"Yup, with Aunt Marie and John. Till Sunday."

"It's my turn for the top bunk, right?"

"Right."

Betsy stood up, threw her arms into the air, and then flopped backward onto her bed. "Capital idea!"

Capital? Oh, yes, Sherlock Holmes. "Capital idea, my dear Watson." Dad must have read another chapter this evening. Megan was now three-quarters awake. "Betsy, did you know that the sun is a star? Betsy?" But Betsy was four-quarters asleep.

Megan stared at the empty place on the floor beside Betsy's bed. She remembered being Betsy's age, waking up in the night and not wanting to go back to sleep because sleeping felt like disappearing. Then she would see Tomorrow Megan on the floor, where Mum had arranged her, ready and waiting for the morning, and it would be okay.

Tomorrow Betsy. She was outgrowing it. But not quite.

Megan rolled out of bed and went to the dresser to pick out an armload of clothes. She sorted through the pile of shoes in the cupboard until she unearthed Betsy's sandals. Then she arranged a little girl on the floor. Underwear, a panda T-shirt, denim skirt, red cardigan, striped kneesocks, sandals, legs crossed. She reached into her own cupboard and brought out her baseball cap for the little girl's head. Then she flicked out the light, sat on the edge of her bed, pulled her knees up inside her nightgown, and stared at the figure.

But Tomorrow Betsy needed something. Megan glanced around the room. The glitter wand was on the bookcase. She slid it out from behind a stuffed lion and leaned over to place it in the little girl's shadowy hand. There. Tomorrow Betsy and her magic wand of power.

CHAPTER SIXTEEN

THE FIRST FERRY TO THE ISLAND WAS VERY EARLY. AS soon as they got on board Mum and Aunt Marie staked out a table and produced their books and a thermos of coffee. "We're on vacation as of now," said Mum. "Here's money for breakfast. Don't fall overboard."

"Ferry breakfast. Capital," said Betsy.

Megan, who had managed to stay more or less asleep during the flurried early-morning packing and the trip to the ferry dock, thought about finding a comfortable bench to curl up on. But Betsy and John were full of plans. Besides, the breakfast smells from the cafeteria were tempting.

They pushed their trays around the cafeteria line and met at a table near the window. Megan had sunshine scrambled eggs. Betsy had a chocolate doughnut and green Jell-o. And John had two glasses of water.

"How come you're not eating?" asked Megan.

"I want to use the money for video games," said John. "They have great ones on the ferry. But Mum thinks that video games stifle creativity and model inappropriate behavior. Anyway, this isn't such a bad breakfast. Wait a minute."

John pushed out past Betsy and went over to the cutlery counter. He came back with a little pillow of ketchup, two lemon slices, a packet of sugar, and two stir sticks. He squeezed the lemon into one glass of water and added sugar. He squeezed the ketchup into the other glass. Then he stirred them both. "There we go, lemonade and tomato juice. All for free."

The tomato juice looked particularly repulsive. "Free but horrible," said Megan.

Betsy, however, was staring in fascination. Megan had the feeling that John had just modeled inappropriate behavior with respect to cafeterias.

Megan and Betsy looked at all the souvenirs in the shop while John blasted evil aliens until he ran out of quarters. Then they went outside, to the back deck, to look for sea gulls and whales. There were plenty of sea gulls, and Betsy spotted several dark waves that might have been whales but weren't.

Megan hung over the rail and stared down into the foaming white wake. With it she tumbled out over the dark green water, time and again.

"Let's play eavesdrop," said John.

Eavesdrop was a game that John had made up. Each player was to go around the ferry and, without being obvious about it, listen in on conversations. Then they were to report back with the funniest line that they had heard anyone say.

"Betsy's too young for eavesdrop," said Megan.

"Am not," said Betsy. "It's one of my best games."

"Okay," said John. "This is a sudden-death round. Five minutes only. Meet back at the kids' playroom."

Megan wandered off to her favorite eavesdrop area in the bookstore. She pretended to browse through a book called *Univalves of the Pacific Northwest* while she waited for the perfect overheard remark. But although there was a buzz of conversation around her, she kept listening to the buzz and not the words. She made one last effort to concentrate and then gave up and stared at a picture of a spotted keyhole limpet. Maybe it was still too early in the morning.

A velvet voice wormed into her head. "Please refrain from starting your vehicle engines until the ferry has docked and vehicles in your lane are requested to begin disembarking. . . ." Yikes. The announcement already. They were almost there. Better head back to Mum and Aunt Marie.

"I won," whispered Betsy as they walked off the ferry.

"Oh yeah, what did you hear?"

"'Jeff has been posted to Flin Flon.'" Betsy giggled and skipped beside Megan. "Flin Flon, Flin Flon, Flin Flon . . ."

Megan looked over at John, who shrugged. "What can I say. She's a natural."

As soon as they arrived at the cottage, Mum sent Betsy down to the beach. "I don't want you around the broken glass," she said, pointing to the smashed window beside the front door.

"I hope there isn't a dead bird inside," said Aunt Marie as she pushed the door open over crunching glass.

"That's why I banished Betsy," said Mum. "You know how she is. I didn't want to spend the whole day arranging a bird funeral."

A careful search revealed no birds, dead or alive, so John got the broom, and Mum and Aunt Marie put on gardening gloves and pulled glass shards out of the window frame. Megan watched.

"Lookit, everybody. Lookit." Betsy was calling from the beach. Megan and John went out to the deck and looked down to see Betsy holding up a big piece of driftwood above her head. "Come on, there's lots!"

110

"Go on, you're excused," said Mum. "We'll just nail some boards over this hole."

John and Megan climbed down to the beach. Betsy was right. There was a whole new supply of driftwood lying in a tangled, seaweedy line on the sand.

"Hey, these are good," said John, pulling pieces free from the tangle. "There's even some long pieces."

"Let's make a house," said Betsy.

John looked at Megan. "Want to?"

Megan shrugged. "Okay."

John propped up the long pieces against the bank, and they all started to collect wood to lay across them for walls.

Megan gathered a few armloads and then it just started to seem like work. She stopped and stared at the bits of wood piled up against the rocky cliff. She tried to make it be a house, but it wouldn't go. It was like one of those optical illusions, a black vase that turns into two white profiles after you've stared at it for a while. But her mind wouldn't make the flip. The pile of wood remained a pile of wood. A heaviness crept up her legs as though she were turning into a lump of wood herself.

She wandered away up the beach, staring down at the sand. A piece of green beach glass, part of a broken pop bottle carved by the sea, glinted in the sunlight, and she picked it up and pocketed it. When she came to the big flat rock they called the table, the incoming tide was lapping at its edges. She drew water pictures on its black surface, and the sun came and erased them. She turned her earrings in her ears.

"*Megan.*" Betsy was coming toward her with a determined look on her face. "Megan, you're not helping. Come *on.*"

"It's not a house anymore," explained Betsy as they returned to the driftwood. "It's a store. We made a security gate so robbers don't steal things."

John was busy hanging strands of slimy, rubbery seaweed over the entrance. "Welcome to Flotsam and Jetsam 'R' Us," he announced. Megan crouched down and pushed her way through the curtain. Inside were arrangements of shells, wood, and pebbles. Betsy followed her in, making it a tight fit.

"What do you want to buy?" asked Betsy.

Megan reached into her pocket and touched the beach glass. It could be an emerald. And then suddenly it couldn't. It was just a hunk of glass. She couldn't even think of anything to say to Betsy except the kind of stupid stuff that grown-ups say when they are only pretending to play. The salt seaweed smell was overpowering and there was a hollowness inside her in the place where her stomach might be. Maybe she just needed lunch. "Betsy, want something to eat?"

Betsy looked offended. "But we just started."

"I know. Sorry. I'll come back later." Megan pushed her way through the seaweed door and headed up to the blackberry patch that lay behind the beach.

The narrow path between the blackberry bushes had a dusty noontime smell. Megan picked her way carefully. How come she wasn't able to play with Betsy and John? It wasn't like not wanting to. It was like not knowing how. Was that what it was like for grown-ups? Was that why they didn't make believe, because they had forgotten how?

She popped three sun-hot blackberries into her mouth and crushed them with her tongue. She was just a step away from the side of the cottage when a stray blackberry branch reached out and grabbed her sock. As she stopped to unhook herself she heard Aunt Marie's voice.

112   "What's the problem?"

Then Mum's. "Oh, it's just that know-it-all stage."

Megan froze.

"She's just so *sure* about everything. I feel like I'm always biting my tongue. Oh, Marie, I wasn't prepared for this."

Marie laughed. "She's just like you were at that age. I remember you laying down the law to father about civil disobedience."

"I know, but it doesn't make her any easier to take. Nobody told me about this part."

Megan clenched her fists and her teeth. She *hated* it when her mum discussed her. What *right* did she have . . .

The wood heaviness in her legs exploded into energy. She turned and ran pounding back along the blackberry path. A branch whipped across her arm. Once out in the open she turned away from the beach and headed toward the woods behind the house. She plunged in, kicking through the undergrowth of ferns and bushes. Her foot caught on a root and she fell, like a tree. She lay still, winded, gulping in the dark green-brown air of the forest. A rough chunk of bark pressed into her cheek. The sunshine and the sounds of the beach were left far behind.

When she sat up, the bark stayed stuck to her cheek. She picked it off, shook the tears from her eyes, and began to talk to her mother. She talked until the words inside her mouth were polished, as perfect and sharp as pine needles.

A thin glowing band of white on a nearby stump caught her attention. A bracket fungus, growing out of the spongy wood like a little lumpy shelf. She pulled it off and turned it over. The underside was clean, untouched, creamy white. She picked up the piece of bark and scratched a jagged brown line across the fungus page. Then she started printing, holding the bark tight in her fist and pressing the bark point deep into the velvety white. "I HATE"—she paused for a second—"THIS. M.H."

Holding the fungus carefully, she got up and pushed through the woods toward the sun. She stood in the shadows at the forest edge and looked back toward the house. Movement. John and Betsy and Aunt Marie were getting out the bikes. She watched as they wobbled up the hill and away. Then she walked down to the beach, across the rocks and sand. She put one foot precisely on the high tide line and threw the fungus as hard as she could, overhand, out across the waves. To Asia.

There. Done.

CHAPTER SEVENTEEN

"Megan!" mum was calling from the deck.

Megan turned, and a breeze caught her hair and blew it across her face. She pushed it away. Yuck. It had bits of leaves and dirt in it.

"Megan! The others have gone into town for ice cream. If you hurry, you can catch them."

"No, it's okay."

"What? I can't hear you."

"It's okay."

Megan trudged up the beach and climbed the stairs to the deck. Mum was lying on a lounge chair.

Megan pushed open the screen door. "I'm going to wash my hair."

Mum put down her book. "Oh, Megan, can you leave it until we get home?"

"But it's dirty."

"It looks okay to me. Just give it a brush."

Megan turned away sharply and clicked her tongue on the roof of her mouth.

"Come on, Megan, chill out." Mum gave a little smile. "It's just the water situation. We don't want to risk a dry well. You know what happened last year."

It was so *revolting* when Mum thought she was being cute by saying things like "chill out." Megan forgot to stay inside herself. "Yes, I know what happened last summer. I *know* a lot of things. I guess I'm a know-it-all. I'm sorry you weren't prepared for it."

Megan walked through the door, letting it slam behind her, stomped through the cottage to the bedroom, heaved that door closed as well, and threw herself on the bottom bunk, facing the wall.

She felt, rather than heard, Mum entering the room. "Megan, I take it you overheard me talking to Marie."

Megan gave one sharp nod to the rough dark wood of the wall.

"Did you think I was talking about you?"

"Yeah, well, who else?"

"Natalie," Mum said quietly.

Megan rolled over and sat up so fast she hit her head on the top bunk. "What?"

"Oh, sweetie, are you all right?" Mum came over and put her hand on Megan's head.

"I'm okay."

Mum sat down on the bed. She had to slump down and put her head sideways to fit. "What I was saying to Marie was about Natalie."

"Don't you like her?"

"I do like her. Very much. But . . . look, it's kind of gloomy in here. Let's go outside." Mum unfolded herself and stood up. "Mind your head."

They sat on the deck, on either end of the lounge. Mum was quiet for a moment. Then she shook her head as though she were shaking something out of her hair. "I *do* like Natalie. And at the beginning that's all there was to it. She was a wonderful surprise, like a present."

"That's when you were crying all the time and being gooey and everything." Anger crept in under Megan's voice.

Mum got pretzel mouth. "Gooey? I guess that's a pretty good description. But then it got more complicated because . . . Oh, I don't know, she's a daughter who's not really a daughter and I don't know if

I'm a mother or a friend or what. And, as I was telling Marie, sometimes she bugs the heck out of me."

"Because she's so smart?"

"Not that really, but she's just so sure of all her opinions. She has positions on everything — politics, the environment. She's probably got a well-thought-out opinion on how to tie your shoelaces. And if I disagree with her, she just rolls over me like a steamroller. I feel flattened. And I know she's got all this education and everything, but, darn it all, sometimes I do know more than she does."

Mum paused and then smiled. "You know I once nearly said to her, 'Listen, I'm old enough to be your mother.' And then I remembered. So mostly I say nothing and then I get irritated and then I feel bad. I'm just swimming around in this stew of emotions."

Megan stared out, past Mum's head, at a high-circling bird. An eagle?

Swimming in stew. Warm and thick and greasy. Pulling your arms through gravy and then your foot would touch a slimy bit of onion. She shuddered.

"What's wrong, you're shivering. Are you cold? Come here." Mom put her arms around Megan and rested her chin on Megan's head. The lounge chair creaked. The circling bird disappeared into the high sky.

"Goodness, this hair could really do with a bath."

"Mu-um." Megan pulled away. "You said it was all right."

"I wasn't paying attention. Come on, I'll wash it for you like at the hairdresser."

They went inside and Mum set some water to boil on the kerosene stove. "Have we got shampoo with us?"

"I always have shampoo." Megan went into the bedroom to dig in her pack.

117

"And we've got a lemon to squeeze over it at the end," Mum called after her.

When she got back, Mum had pulled the table up to the sink and rolled a beach towel into a bolster. She helped Megan climb up onto the blue-and-yellow oilcloth.

The table creaked and wobbled a bit, but it was surprisingly comfortable to lie back on the towel cushion. Mum spread Megan's hair out in a fan and ran her finger gently across Megan's forehead. "You did give yourself a nasty crack. I think you might be outgrowing the bunk beds." Mum poured a dipper of water over Megan's head. "Warm enough?"

"Hmmm."

Megan closed her eyes. Shampoo, rinse, shampoo, rinse. Mum was slower than Nicholas the hairdresser, and gentler. Megan floated, giving her head away to someone else to take care of.

Mum started talking as though she were in the middle of a conversation. "But you know what the strangest thing is? For years after I gave up Natalie for adoption I used to invent stories about her. How she was learning to walk and starting kindergarten and all that. Over the years I created this make-believe person."

"Like Brunty?"

Mum laughed. "Brunty! That's exactly it. I haven't thought of Brunty in years. Do you remember the time you made us get a booster seat for Brunty in that Chinese restaurant?"

Megan shook her head. What *did* she remember about Brunty? A vague feeling of sitting in the bath and seeing Brunty on the edge of the tub.

118

"And then there was the time that Brunty made you bury Talking Doll in the compost bin. Brunty had a very large personality for someone who was invisible."

Megan smiled. Mum remembered more about Brunty than she did. All in the story together.

The lemon juice ran over Megan's head like cool fingers.

"Anyway, when the real Natalie turned up, one of the things that happened was that I had to say good-bye to the imaginary child who disappeared. And I missed her. Silly, eh, missing someone who never existed?"

Megan reached into her pocket and fingered the piece of green glass that wasn't an emerald.

She felt the rough corner of the towel circling her ears and then Mum's hand on the back of her neck. She sat up and Mum wound a towel turban around her head.

"Come on, you can dry your hair in the sun."

Megan lay on the deck and brushed her hair out over the edge, upside down. The sun warmed the back of her neck, and the sharp smell of lemon tickled her nose. She heard a soft *fwap* and she flipped her hair right side up and turned around. Mum was fast asleep, one arm flopping beside the lounge chair, and her book lying open on the deck, its pages riffling in the breeze.

Megan picked up the book, stretched, and wandered inside. She did a headstand on the fat arm of the couch and then toppled over onto the soft cushions and did a somersault, finishing up with her chin on the arm next to the window. On the windowsill lay the blue fish float, in its nest of net and shells.

She picked it up and looked through it, out the window. Blue distorto world. She held it up to the sun. The little pockmarks on its surface reminded her of something. The moon, that was it. It was like the craters of the moon, seen through a telescope.

Natalie would see that. Except she wouldn't say, "*the* moon." She would say, "*our* moon," because she thought about so many other moons and suns.

Megan rolled the cool ball along the inside of her arm, across her blackberry-bush injury, a path of tiny red dots. She thought of the float coming loose from some fisherman's net near Japan and floating thousands of miles across the ocean, bobbing along blue in the sun or tossed in waves. Tossed off the white edge of waves but never breaking. Passing by driftwood and seaweed and floating birds until it reached the shore and hid under a salal bush to wait for her.

My moon, our moon. Of course. A perfect wedding present.

Triing. The sounds of a bicycle bell and laughing voices floated in through the window. A wedding present from her, and from Betsy. They could wrap it in layers and layers of tissue paper and put it in a big box. They could hide it one last time.

They wouldn't tell Mum. It would be a surprise. A secret. Just a short-kept one. The best kind.